中国寓言故事选英译

A Selection of Chinese Fables Translated into English

霍红　刘猛　编译

中国海洋大学出版社
· 青岛 ·

图书在版编目（CIP）数据

中国寓言故事选英译／霍红，刘猛编译 . -- 青岛：
中国海洋大学出版社，2024.12. -- ISBN 978-7-5670
-3902-5

Ⅰ. I277.4

中国国家版本馆 CIP 数据核字第 20245HV686 号

出版发行	中国海洋大学出版社		
社　　址	青岛市香港东路 23 号	邮政编码	266071
出 版 人	刘文菁		
网　　址	http://pub.ouc.edu.cn		
订购电话	0532-82032573（传真）		
责任编辑	邵成军	电　　话	0532-85902533
印　　制	青岛海蓝印刷有限责任公司		
版　　次	2024 年 12 月第 1 版		
印　　次	2024 年 12 月第 1 次印刷		
成品尺寸	170 mm ×230 mm		
印　　张	16.00		
字　　数	140 千		
印　　数	1—1 000		
定　　价	129.00 元		

译者简介

霍红

　　2001 年成都理工大学英语专业毕业,获文学学士学位;2005 年澳大利亚莫纳什大学国际英语教学专业毕业,获教育学硕士学位;2013 年 12 月至 2014 年 12 月在美国俄克拉何马州立大学英语系访学;2015 年上海外国语大学英语语言文学专业毕业,获博士学位;2015 至 2021 年,于扬州大学文学院做博士后。现为扬州大学外国语学院副教授、硕士生导师。主要学术兴趣包括文学翻译、语用学及二语习得。系江苏省翻译工作者协会会员。主持江苏省教育厅哲学社会科学研究项目 1 项,主持校级科研项目多项,出版教材 2 部,出版《海棠依旧·霍红双语诗集选》自创自译中英双语格律诗著作 1 部,出版《英韵经典唐诗百首》译著 1 部,多篇翻译作品在《英语世界》等期刊发表。

The Author's Profile

Huo Hong, who received a Bachelor's degree in English literature from Chengdu University of Technology in 2001, a Master's degree in TESOL from Monash University, Australia in 2005, a doctoral degree in English language and literature from Shanghai International Studies University in 2015 and who was a visiting scholar to the English department of Oklahoma State University, the US from the December 2013 to that of 2014 and was doing postdoctoral research at College of Humanities of Yangzhou University from 2015 to 2021, is now an associate professor of College of International Studies of Yangzhou University, who supervises postgraduates and whose academic interest covers literary translation, pragmatics and second language acquisition. As a member of Jiangsu Translators Association, she is found productive in books and research papers, has undertaken one provincial project funded by Educational Department of Jiangsu Province and was involved in compiling two textbooks. Keen on translating traditional Chinese poems though, she has translated some literary works such as English-translated essays published in *The English World*. More than what relates to her career, she is a poet who has had a poem selection of her own published, namely *Gone and Go On* in both Chinese and English, with her translated work *Classic Tang Poems in English Rhyme* lately published.

译者简介

刘猛

　　2001 年成都理工大学英语专业毕业，获文学学士学位；2005 年澳大利亚莫纳什大学国际英语教学专业毕业，获教育学硕士学位；2014 年上海外国语大学翻译学专业毕业，获文学博士学位；2017 年 8 月至 2018 年 8 月赴美国夏威夷大学教育学院访学；2015 年 1 月至 2021 年 6 月在扬州大学文学院做博士后。现为扬州大学外国语学院副教授、硕士生导师，江苏省翻译工作者协会理事。主要学术兴趣包括口笔译理论与实践、二语习得。主持教育部专业学位案例库项目 1 项、江苏省教育厅哲学社会科学研究项目 1 项，参与国家社科基金项目 4 项，主持多项校级科研项目，出版教材 6 部，在省级及以上期刊发表学术论文 10 余篇。所指导的学生多次在全国各类英语口笔译比赛中获一等奖。多次承担各类会议口译、笔译工作。

The Author's Profile

Liu Meng, who received a Bachelor's degree in English literature from Chengdu University of Technology in 2001, a Master's degree in TESOL from Monash University, Australia in 2005, a doctoral degree in interpretation and translation from Shanghai International Studies University in 2014 and who was a visiting scholar to the Department of Education, Hawaii University, the US from the August of 2017 to that of 2018 and was doing postdoctoral research at College of Humanities of Yangzhou University from the January of 2015 to the June of 2021, is now an associate professor of College of International Studies of Yangzhou University, who supervises postgraduates and whose academic interest falls on interpretation and translation and second language acquisition. Cast in the multiple role, he is found with a wide range of harvests—having received a grant from China Professional-degree Case Center under Ministry of Education, having completed a Philosophical Science Fund Project granted by Educational Department of Jiangsu Province, being involved in four National Social Science Fund Projects, having been a holder of several university-granted fund projects, textbooks, publications as well as a plurality of first prizes in teaching or instructing students for interpretation or translation competition. Nonetheless, as a member of Jiangsu Translators Association, he retains his expertise in interpretation and translation by interpreting at a great number of conferences and translating a diversity of works.

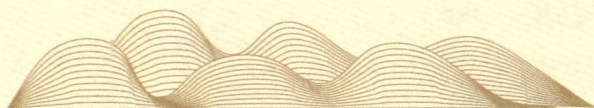

序

  中国传统文化浩浩汤汤，不仅含蕴于诗词歌赋中，也含蕴于神话、寓言以及一些民间故事中。在我国悠久的历史长河中，自春秋、战国，到秦、汉，再到元、明、清，每一个朝代皆孕生了经典的寓言。它们是中华文化的一种独特的存在形式，是对中华文化、中华精神、中华智慧的引领与传承。一些寓言故事，如《拔苗助长》《愚公移山》，由于其承载的深刻寓意而成为中华智慧的精粹，在人的学习以及成长过程中都具有很重要的教育意义。

  寓言是一种以假托的人物或自然物的拟人手法来说明某个道理的文学作品，或反映了社会面貌和政治现实，或给人以智慧，或示与世人以处世的法则，是一种用以讽刺或警示世人的说理性故事。寓言作为一种文学体裁，篇幅短小，语言精练，富含哲理，是人们认识社会、明白事理以及品味人性的经验和智慧的结晶。

  每个民族都有其诗歌、神话、寓言、典故以及民间故事，它们共同建构了这个民族的文化宝库，也是该民族的文化精华和智慧所在。负载着诸多文化信息的中国诗歌、神话、寓言以及民间故事，不仅是中国人了解中华民族文化的金钥匙，也是世界了解中国与中华文化的窗口。"世界上历史悠久而又传承至今的传统文化有三大体系。一是发源于地中海区域的欧洲文化，一是发源于印度的南亚中东文化，一是发源于中国大陆的东亚文化。世界寓言与世界文化相适应,也有这样的三大体系,即印度南亚中东寓言体系,希腊欧洲寓言体系,中国东亚寓言体系。"(陈蒲清,2007:38)

在这三大寓言体系中,除以中国古代寓言为代表的中国东亚寓言体系而外,最为人熟知的便是"伊索寓言"了。以《伊索寓言》这本书为例,其中收录了典型的欧洲寓言,以拟人化动物为主角,主要讽刺不平等或不良的社会现象,也涉及道德教育、伦理等内容。现流行的《伊索寓言》版本包含百则寓言,与中国古代寓言相比具有相似之处与不同之处。

两者的相似之处在于以下方面:第一,篇幅多短小,语言精练;第二,富含人生经验和智慧、做人的道理以及哲理;第三,以拟人化动物为主角。两者也有不同之处,主要在于以下方面:第一,故事来源不同,中国的寓言故事主要出自中华典籍著作,故事由诸子学者讲述,而伊索寓言为古代希腊奴隶伊索所著或收集的故事集,后又加入印度、阿拉伯以及基督教故事;第二,中国的寓言故事中,完全以动物为主角的少之又少,多数以人与物的互动生成故事情节,以达到警示或教育的目的,而伊索寓言故事的主角以拟人化的动物为主;第三,寓意不同,中国的寓言故事多为历史人物故事,其寓意主要是宣传政治哲学主张以及处世哲学,而伊索寓言多讽刺人性、人心的阴暗;第四,应用差异,中国的寓言故事生成了丰富的四字成语,现今仍广泛使用,如"朝三暮四""井底之蛙""杞人忧天""邯郸学步",而伊索寓言的故事虽广为流传,却很少作为成语使用。

本书选译的篇目主要来自《列子》《庄子》《战国策》《韩非子》《吕氏春秋》《新序》以及《雪涛故事》,共选译108篇,其中一部分寓言是对著名翻译家杨宪益、戴乃迭夫妇所译的《中国古代寓言选》所收录寓言的重译。随着中国文化走出去的战略开启,中国寓言故事,这一与伊索寓言具有同样教育意义、承载中国文化的故事,应追求更为严肃的译文以推动其在接受过高等教育的人群中的传播。本译作仿《伊索寓言》,在原文本结尾处附上故事"寓意",以帮助读者理解故事中所阐述的道理以及对人生的可能指导。

我们希望《中国寓言故事选英译》能够成为中国文化走向世界的一艘舰艇，跟随时代的洪流，驶向世界文化的海洋，让承载着绚烂的中华文明、中华智慧的它被轻轻打开、细细翻读。

本书获得中国海洋大学出版社邵成军主任的大力支持以及扬州大学出版基金资助，特此感谢。

霍 红　刘 猛

2024 年 7 月 18 日于扬州

Preface

Not only does the traditional Chinese culture stream forward along the torrents of the times in the form of poetry and lyrics, but it is harboured in myths, fables and folklores as well. From the Spring and Autumn Period and the Warring States Period to the Qin and Han Dynasties to the Yuan, Ming and Qing Dynasties in the long river of history, every and each dynasty bred classic fables, which exist as the iconology of the Chinese civilization, leading and carrying forward the Chinese culture, the Chinese spirit and the Chinese wisdom. A number of fables, which have made the quintessence of the Chinese wit owing to their thought-provoking morals, are of great significance in the process of personal growth.

The fable, which bases itself on satire and warning of precipice in human world, brings forth truism or a moral through invented figures and/or personified animals or objects, either reflecting social realities or allowing people wisdom or showing the rules of interaction between social beings. Seen mostly short in length, concise in language, and philosophic in theme, the fable, as a literary genre, is a combined work of both human experience and wisdom that improves one's understanding of the society, the way to deal with people and human nature.

Every nation has its own poems, myths, fables, literary allusions and folklores, which work in concert to construct the nation's trove of cultural treasure and which the Chinese cultural quintessence and wisdom are based upon. Affording the Chinese people a key to their own culture, the Chinese poems, myths, fables and so on loaded with a mass of cultural information lead people of the entire world to the access to China and its culture. "The three systems of world cultures with a long history passed down to the present day are: European culture originating in the Mediterranean region, South Asia/Middle East culture originating in India, and East Asian culture that started on the mainland of China. Accordingly, world fables are divided into three corresponding categories: European, South Asian/Middle Eastern, and East Asian." (Chen Puqing, 2007:38)

Apart from the Chinese fables that are a focused display of the East Asian ones, the most widely-known are Aesop's fables. Exemplified in stories collected in *Aesop's Fables*, the book has included classical ancient Greek fables, which satirically indicates the phenomenon of social inequality and villainy through the protagonists of personified animals or objects, involving ethical issues. The current version of *Aesop's Fables*, in which around a hundred fables are involved, has similarities to and differences from the ancient Chinese fables.

Similarities exist as follows. First, both come short in length and concise in language usage; second, both embody morals and philosophies of life by bringing out life experience and wisdom; third, both are found with protagonists as personified animals or objects. Differences are found as on the following list. First, they are of differed origins. The Chinese fables, for the most part, come from classic ancient works by famed scholars, philosophers and thinkers while *Aesop's Fables* is a collection of fables composed or gathered by Aesop, said to be a slave, with Indian, Arab or Christian stories added in. Second, personified animals or objects are rarely found as main characters in the Chinese fables, the plot of which develops largely through man and animals or objects while the protagonists in *Aesop's Fables* come in the form to the contrary. Third, they come up with different morals. The Chinese fables that often are concerned with historical figures are intended to expound on some political philosophy or philosophy of life while Aesop's fables mostly satirize and reveal the villainy of humanity. Forth, they are to different uses. Most of the Chinese fables gave rise to idioms of four Chinese characters, which remain in wide use nowadays, while despite its wide spread, Aesop's fables rarely come to idioms for daily use.

The English-translated fables in this book are chosen primarily from *Lie Tzu*, *Zhuang Tzu*, *Warring States Anecdotes*, *Han Fei Tzu*, *Spring and Autumn by Lv Buwei*, *New Discourse* and *Stories of Xuetao*, with a total of 108 fables, some of which are re-translated versions of the fables in *Ancient Chinese Fables* translated by Yang Xianyi and Gladys Yang into English and the rest of which are chosen from the above mentioned and some other classic books. With the trend of Chinese culture launched, the Chinese fables, whose educational significance can be compared with that of Aesop's fables and which bear the Chinese cultural elements, should seek spread among adult readers with higher education. This book of *A Selection of Chinese Fables Translated into English*, patterned after *Aesop's Fables*, has each fable followed by an "Application" aimed to lead the readers to the right understanding of the morals given by the story.

With great sincerity, we are in the hope that *A Selection of Chinese Fables Translated into English* will be able to ride the torrents of the times, flowing into the ocean of the world cultures, make a culture-loaded ship heading to the world, and draw readers to open and read it.

With greatest sincerity, we herein extend our gratitude to Shao Chengjun, executive editor of China Ocean University Press for his affirmation and to Yangzhou University for the Publishing Grant.

Huo Hong & Liu Meng
July 18th, 2024 in Yangzhou

目录 CONTENTS

1

杞人忧天

　　杞国有人忧天地崩坠，身亡所寄，废寝食者。又有忧彼之所忧者，因往晓之，曰："天，积气耳，亡处亡气。若屈伸呼吸，终日在天中行止，奈何忧崩坠乎？"

　　其人曰："天果积气，日月星宿，不当坠耶？"

　　晓之者曰："日月星宿，亦积气中之有光耀者，只使坠，亦不能有所中伤。"

　　其人曰："奈地坏何？"

　　晓者曰："地，积块耳，充塞四虚，亡处亡块。若躇步跐蹈，终日在地上行止，奈何忧其坏？"

　　其人舍然大喜，晓之者亦舍然大喜。

——《列子》

警言

　　不要毫无根据地忧虑和担心，空耗自己的情绪，患得患失。与其为一些虚幻的可能而忧心，不如脚踏实地，将时间和精力花在自身能够把握的事情上。

A Man Being Overalarmed

Once upon a time, there lived a man in the state of Qi, who was apprehensive of the chance that the sky and the earth might collapse leaving no space for him to sustain himself thereupon, to find himself on reduced sleep and diet. Another man who was concerned about the first man's apprehension went to him with an intention to relieve him of his worries. "The sky is no more than lifted air that is nonexistent nowhere. You bend down, stretch yourself, inhale and exhale, moving about in the air. Why do you fear it's going to fall?"

"Given that the sky is indeed air, won't the sun, the moon and the constellation descend from the heights?" doubted the apprehensive one.

"What you mentioned are those in the air which give out light. Even if they drop, there is little occasion where harm will be done," replied the latter one.

"What if the ground caves in?" enquired the former one.

"The ground is but chunked earth, which is all around, far and near, no earthen chunk found nowhere. You stroll, walk, tread, and scamper, moving about all day long—what makes you fear it's going to sink? " said the latter.

The man, as relieved of a heavy load, went overwhelmed with elation. So did the other man.

——from *Lie Tzu*

Application

Stop letting groundless apprehension consume your mental energy in vain or being swayed by what to gain and what to lose. You had better lay your focused time and vigour on what you are able to have a grasp of than show meaningless concern for something you are not enabled to seize upon.

朝三暮四

宋有狙公者,爱狙,养之成群,能解狙之意,狙亦得公之心。损其家口,充狙之欲。

俄而匮焉,将限其食。恐众狙之不驯于己也,先诳之曰:"与若芧,朝三而暮四,足乎?"众狙皆起而怒。

俄而曰:"与若芧,朝四而暮三,足乎?"众狙皆伏而喜。

—— 《列子》

警 言

圣人用智慧来笼络愚人,就像养猴老翁用其智慧来笼络猴子一样。名义和实际都不亏损,却能使它们欢喜或愤怒。

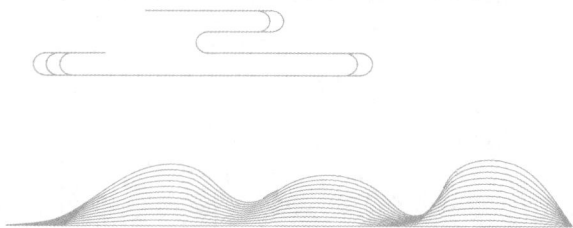

Three in the Morning and Four in the Evening

A monkey-raising man in the state of Song was fond of, kept a massive herd of and had a good knowledge of monkeys, who in turn understood every intention of his.

He deducted his family's ration of food, with which to satisfy the monkeys' dietary aspiration. It wasn't long before his limited storage of food couldn't suffice, which led to a cut-down share for the monkeys. He deceived them lest they refuse the arrangement of a reduced share. "I can afford you three chestnuts each morning and four each evening," he announced. "Is it fine with you?"

All of the monkeys sprang to rage against him. After a while he made another offer.

"Four in the morning and three in the evening," he enquired, "is that good enough?"

With these words to the ear, the herd of monkeys agreed with joy.

——from *Lie Tzu*

Application

The sage wins over the fool with his wit the same way that the old monkey-raising man won over the monkeys. With no seeming or impressive loss, they have been rendered joyful or wrathful.

燕人还国

燕人生于燕，长于楚，及老而还本国。

过晋国，同行者诳之，指城曰："此燕国之城。"其人愀然变容。指社曰："此若里之社。"乃喟然而叹。指舍曰："此若先人之庐。"乃涓然而泣。指垄曰："此若先人之冢。"

其人哭不自禁。同行者哑然大笑，曰："予昔绐若，此晋国耳。"其人大惭。

及至燕，真见燕国之城社，真见先人之庐冢，悲心更微。

——《列子》

警 言

同样的外界条件刺激，第一次提及时激起强烈的情感；第二次提及时所激起的情感便不那么强烈。在日常生活中，重要的事情不是说了三遍便一定能够引起听者的注意，反之，一而再再而三地说起，可能会令听者对所听的事情不那么重视了。

Going Back to Hometown

A man was born in the state of Yan, grew up in the state of Chu and returned to his home state of Yan at his old age.

When he was passing by the state of Jin, one of his companions played a joke on him.

"That's the city wall of Yan," said the fellow, pointing to the wall.

Hearing the words, the man took on a sad look, overwhelmed with a strong feeling of homesickness.

"That's the village god temple of your hometown," said the fellow again, pointing to the temple.

With these words to his ear, the man sighed a long sorrowful sigh.

"Those are the houses where your ancestors ever lived," said the fellow a third time, pointing to the houses.

When hearing of this, the man was stirred to unstoppable tears.

"That's your great grandfather's tomb," said the fellow a fourth time, pointing to a roadside mound.

Upon these words, the man could not help bursting into loud cries. At the sight of this, his companion laughed so good a laugh.

"I've just played tricks on you. This land we are passing is but that of Jin," clarified the fellow.

Knowing what it was really like, the man was struck by a feeling of embarrassment, which he derived from his gullibility. When he caught sight of the walls that ran around his four sides, god temples, the old houses and even the tombs in the land of Yan, his distress but weakened.

——from *Lie Tzu*

Application

In terms of the same trigger for attention, when referred to for the first time, it stirs a heart to the strongest degree. Referred to for the second time, it lessens the degree to which it moves a heart. Therefore, in our daily life, a thing repeated three times may not necessarily draw the listener's attention. On the contrary, when said over and over again, it will somehow evade the listener's mind.

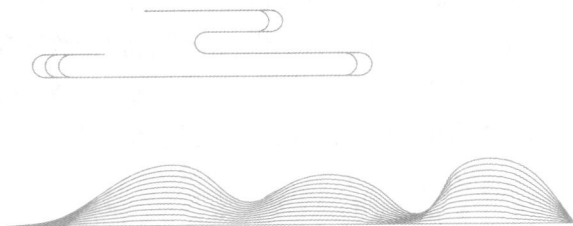

愚公移山

太行、王屋二山，方七百里，高万仞；本在冀州之南，河阳之北。

北山愚公者，年且九十，面山而居。惩山北之塞，出入之迂也，聚室而谋曰："吾与汝毕力平险，指通豫南，达于汉阴，可乎？"杂然相许。其妻献疑曰："以君之力，曾不能损魁父之丘，如太行、王屋何？且焉置土石？"杂曰："投诸渤海之尾，隐土之北。"遂率子孙荷担者三夫，叩石垦壤，箕畚运于渤海之尾。邻人京城氏之孀妻有遗男，始龀，跳往助之。寒暑易节，始一反焉。

河曲智叟笑而止之曰："甚矣，汝之不惠！以残年余力，曾不能毁山之一毛，其如土石何？"北山愚公长息曰："汝心之固，固不可彻，曾不若孀妻弱子。虽我之死，有子存焉。子又生孙，孙又生子；子又有子，子又有孙；子子孙孙无穷匮也，而山不加增，何苦而不平？"河曲智叟亡以应。

操蛇之神闻之，惧其不已也，告之于帝。帝感其诚，命夸娥氏二子负二山，一厝朔东，一厝雍南。自此，冀之南，汉之阴，无陇断焉。

——《列子》

警言

不要低估劳动人民改造自然的气魄。具有设定远大目标的气魄，认定一个目标，向着目标坚持不懈地努力，如此则能实现一番他人认为不可为之的大事业。可见，雄心壮志、坚定的信念以及矢志不渝的努力对于事业的成功具有十分重要的意义。

Old Fool Moving Mountains

The Taihang and Wangwu Mountains, some 350 kilometres in circumference and hundreds of thousands of feet high, used to stand south of Jizhou and north of Heyang County.

An old man aged nearly ninety, whose house sat north of these mountains, was perceived as foolish, known as Old Fool. The mountains, as a massive block, obliged the old man and his family to make a detour in and out, which thereby led to his call of a family meeting. "Suppose we strive to the utmost of our strength to level the mountains, and we will be able to have an open pass through the south of Yuzhou (most of today's Henan Province) to the bank of the Han River." To this all agreed except his wife.

"With your strength, you cannot remove the Kuifu Hummock even a trace," she rejoined, "and what can you do with these two high mountains? Besides, where would you dump the earth and stones?"

"We can dump them north of Yintu into the sea," the others replied.

Old Fool, together with his son and grandson thereafter, the three of them carrying shoulder poles, gouged rocks, dug up the earth and conveyed them in baskets to the sea. A widowed woman, whose late husband was named Jingcheng, and his posthumous son, the baby teeth of whom had just started to come off, went to give help of their own accord. Only with the passage of a summer and a winter, was a trip to and fro completed.

The wise old man who dwelt at the river bend, known as Old Wise, scoffing at their earnest attempt, went all out to stop them.

"Enough of this folly!" he exclaimed. "How stupid it is of you to try to do this! Old and weak, you cannot in any likelihood remove a fraction of the mountains, let alone so goodly an amount of earth and stones."

9

"You have an obstinate mind that does not open itself to our senses. You have even no sense of the widow's and the little one's. Dead as I go, I shall leave behind my son, who will leave behind his son and grandson, my offspring to be had from generation to generation. In the circumstance where the mountains won't grow larger, how can't they be razed to the ground?" Old Fool heaved a long sigh.

Informed of the foolish old man's determined project, God of mountains reported this to the emperor in heaven lest it be long before the gouging and digging came to an end. Stirred by the man's resolution, the emperor in charge of all gods bade two sons of Kua'e, God of Power, move the two mountains, one to deposit at Shuofang (today's north of Shanxi Province) and the other to lay at Yongzhou (between Shaanxi Province and Shanxi Province). From then on, at the Han River south of Hebei Province there came no bar to those who would make trips.

——from *Lie Tzu*

Application

As can be expected, the daring of the people to struggle for the reshaping of nature should never be underestimated. Equip yourself with the courage to set an ambitious goal, identify a specific aim and persevere in pursuit of it, and then you will be able to accomplish an impressive undertaking deemed in others' eyes as unachievable. It is to the general understanding that ambition, unswerving determination and persistent exertion of toil cast themselves in the decisive role of leading to the achievement in an undertaking.

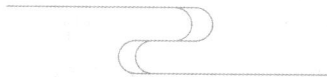

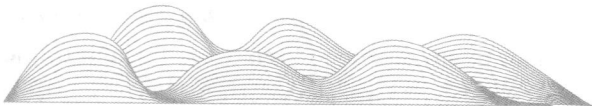

夸父追日

夸父不量力，欲追日影，逐之于隅谷之际。渴欲得饮，赴饮河、渭。河渭不足，将走北饮大泽。未至，道渴而死。弃其杖，尸膏肉所浸，生邓林。邓林弥广数千里焉。

—— 《列子》

警 言

人生的追求若虚无肤泛、不够实际，则穷尽其力地付出也难以达成目标。进行正确的自我认知，准确地评估自身的能力，量力而行，以免走向悲剧的结局。

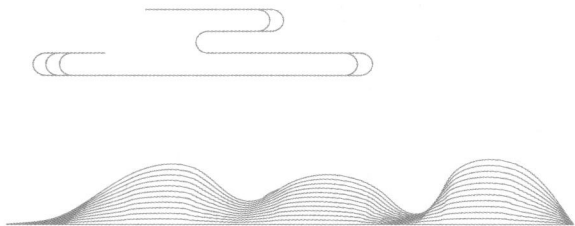

Quafoo in Pursuit of the Sun

Regardless of his strength, Quafoo, who was disposed to chase after the sun, kept after it to where the sun set in an outlying valley. When he thirsted, he took to the Yellow River and the Weihe River for a drink of water. If the water in the two rivers failed to suffice, he was going to head north to the grand marsh for some water. Before he was able to reach the sun, he died of thirst. His deserted cane, immersed in the fat and blood converted from his body, evolved into a grove of peach trees, which stretched and stretched to a wide area of several thousand *li* around.

——from *Lie Tzu*

Application

If in void, impractical pursuit, you will barely be able to achieve your goal even with effort not to spare. A true knowledge of yourself, precise measurement of your own ability and capacity-based practice jointly contribute to the avoidance of leading to a tragical end.

两小儿辩日

孔子东游,见两小儿辩斗。问其故。

一儿曰:"我以日始出时去人近,而日中时远也。"

一儿以日初出远,而日中时近也。

一儿曰:"日初出大如车盖,及日中,则如盘盂:此不为远者小而近者大乎?"

一儿曰:"日初出沧沧凉凉,及其日中如探汤:此不为近者热而远者凉乎?"

孔子不能决也。

两小儿笑曰:"孰为汝多知乎?"

—— 《列子》

警 言

知识无穷,学无止境。孔子作为中国古代著名的哲学家、思想家,仍能实事求是,敢于承认自己学识的不足,这才是追求真理应该具备的精神。独立思考、大胆质疑更是进行研究不可或缺的科学精神。

Two Boys' Discussion About the Sun

On his travel to the east, Confucius, who ran across two boys in heated discussion directed at the sun, came up to them and enquired what their argument was aimed at.

"I hold that the sun is close to us at sunrise while far at midday," said one of the two boys.

The other was of the opinion that it was far as the sun rises while close in the middle of the day.

"The sun looks as big as a carriage top and grows to the size of a plate: isn't it that what's far appears small and what's near large?" argued one of them.

"The temperature climbs from low at sunrise to high at midday: isn't it that what's near feels hot and what's far cold?" the other contradicted.

Confucius was unable to umpire their discussion.

"Who said you are a learned scholar?" the two little ones smiled.

——from *Lie Tzu*

Application

As the ocean of knowledge goes infinite, one can never come to an end in terms of learning. As one of the major ideologists and the greatest philosophers, Confucius who calls a spade a spade affords to admit his lack of certain knowledge, which is a demonstration of his most valuable scholarly quality to learn in pursuit of truth. Equally important is the capacity for independent and critical thinking, which is an indispensable element to a researcher.

薛谭学讴

薛谭学讴于秦青，未穷青之技，自谓尽之，遂辞归。秦青弗止，饯于郊衢。抚节悲歌，声振林木，响遏行云。薛谭乃谢求反，终身不敢言归。

——《列子》

警 言

这则寓言告诉我们：学无止境，不可稍有成绩就沾沾自喜；浅尝辄止不是学习之道，要不断钻研，孜孜不倦。

Learning to Sing

Xue Tan, who was a famous singer himself, had learnt to sing under the tutelage of Qin Qing, a widely-recognized singer of his times. Not until Xue Tan had mastery of all Qin Qing's art, did he believe that he had acquired all singing techniques, which led him to a request to go home. Showing no concern for his leaving, the teacher saw him off by the main road in the suburbs, where a farewell dinner was ready. During the dinner, the singing teacher, hand beating the bamboo-made musical instrument, sang an excited song, whose echoes stirred the trees in the woods, resonating between and stilling the floating clouds. When the beautiful notes danced their way to his ears, Xue Tan could not wait to make a hearty apology to his teacher, asking to remain under his guidance. From then on, this student who learnt to sing never ventured even once to say of leaving school for home.

——from *Lie Tzu*

Application

This fable warns us that we always can better ourselves in terms of learning, which stops us from complacency for what we have achieved up to now. A little knowledge of something is not the right way to learning. The more, the better. As a student, one should go to greatest strenghs to have a deepened knowledge or understanding on the adventure to your learning destination.

纪昌学箭

甘蝇，古之善射者，彀弓而兽伏鸟下。弟子名飞卫，学射于甘蝇，而巧过其师。纪昌者，又学射于飞卫。

飞卫曰："尔先学不瞬，而后可言射矣。"

纪昌归，偃卧其妻之机下，以目承牵挺。二年之后，虽锥末倒眦，而不瞬也。以告飞卫。

飞卫曰："未也，必学视而后可。视小如大，视微如著，而后告我。"

昌以氂悬虱于牖，南面而望之。旬日之间，浸大也；三年之后，如车轮焉。以睹馀物，皆丘山也。乃以燕角之弧，朔蓬之簳射之，贯虱之心，而悬不绝。以告飞卫。

飞卫高蹈拊膺曰："汝得之矣！"

——《列子》

警言

学习任何一种技能或知识，坚实的基本功是能力形成的基础。这就如同练武术，首先要练蹲马步，要练体能，甚至练劈柴，之后再学习各种武术动作。没有前面几项的锻炼，武术的动作则成了花架子，没有力量，没有攻击力。学习京剧，要先会吊嗓子；学习一门外语，要先多积累词汇、多阅读，才能开口讲这门外语以及用这种语言进行翻译和写作。

Ji Chang Learning to Shoot

Gan Ying, a most skilled archer, brought beasts and birds down onto the ground so long as he drew his bow to the full extent. He had a student, Fei Wei, whose skills outdid his teacher's. Ji Chang came then to Fei Wei, asking to be his student.

"Practise keeping your eyes unstirred before you say of shooting to me," said Fei Wei.

Arriving home, Ji Chang lay down under his wife's loom, his eyes gazed upon the pedal that went up and down, up and down. He practised and practised. Two years later, his eyes could manage to remain unperturbed in case that the tip of an awl stabbed at them. Ji Chang thereby reported this to Fei Wei.

"Not good enough yet. You must practise your eyesight well before it suffices for shooting," this skilled archer of Fei Wei maintained. "That is, don't come to me until you see tiny things as well as large ones and the subtle as well as the marked."

Upon these words, Ji Chang then tied a louse to a cowhair, hung it at the window, and fixed his eyes on it, facing southward. With the passage of around ten days, the louse looked bigger. It looked bigger and larger to Ji Chang until it looked as large as a wheel three years after, when his eyes laid on something else, it appeared as impressive as the hill. He thereupon held up the bow made of an ox horn in one hand and the arrow made of bamboo in the other, let the arrow go at the heart of the louse, and the cowhair to which the louse was tied was not severed. This he reported to Fei Wei.

Elated at Chang's report, Fei Wei flew into raptures, clapping his chest, and exclaimed, "You've got the hang of shooting!"

——from *Lie Tzu*

Application

In order to master a certain technique or knowledge, solid foundation to be laid is the very first step to the development of ability. To be specific, to do martial arts, you should first do a martial-arts squat for a length of time before you proceed to the movements. Without practice at the basic level, the movements would be just taking the martial-arts form without martial-arts quality. To learn to sing Peking opera, you should exercise your voice for prolonged time before you are allowed to sing. Also, to learn a foreign language, vocabulary and a good deal of reading are what you are supposed to be involved in, based on which you will be able to speak the language with fluency and precision, be a good translator and write good essays.

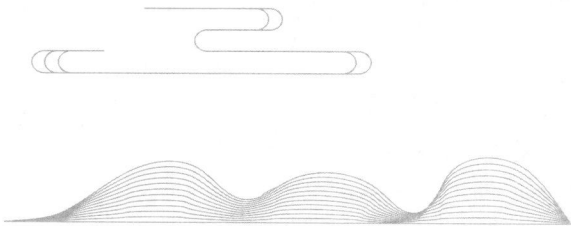

歧路亡羊

杨子之邻人亡羊,即率其党,又请杨子之竖追之。

杨子曰:"嘻!亡一羊何追者之众?"

邻人曰:"多歧路。"

既反,问:"获羊乎?"

曰:"亡之矣。"

曰:"奚亡之?"

曰:"歧路之中又有歧焉,吾不知所之,所以反也。"

杨子戚然变容,不言者移时,不笑者竟日。

门人怪之,请曰:"羊,贱畜;又非夫子之有,而损言笑者,何哉?"

杨子不答。门人不获所命。弟子孟孙阳出以告心都子……

心都子曰:"大道以多歧亡羊,学者以多方丧生。学非本不同,非本不一,而末异若是。唯归同反一,为亡得丧。子长先生之门,习先生之道,而不答先生之况也,哀哉!"

——《列子》

警言

当情况纷繁复杂时,若不能掌握正确的方向,则难免误入歧途或一无所获。

A Sheep Going Astray at a Fork in the Road

Yang Tzu's neighbour lost a sheep, led his men to seek for it and solicited Yang Tzu's boy servant to join in the search.

"What!" exclaimed Yang Tzu. "Why do you have so many men look for one sheep?"

"Several bypaths for it to take," the neighbour responded.

"Have you found the sheep?" Yang Tzu enquired of the neighbour as he returned, who answered that they had not. "Why have you failed to get it back?" was Yang Tzu's enquiry thereupon. "Bypaths lead to more bypaths. Not knowing which to follow, we just turned around on our way back," as the reply went.

When Yang Tzu heard his neighbour's response, distress took possession of his countenance and he remained in silence for prolonged hours, wearing no smile for as long as an entire day.

Wondering at the display of their teacher's dismay, his pupils remarked questioningly, "A sheep is a mere trifle, which is not even your possession. Why on earth should you subside to fewer utterances and absence of smile for a day?"

No answer was given by Yang Tzu, whose pupils were somewhat confounded with it. One of them, named Mengsun Yang, went out for Xindou Tzu to inform him of what had happened.

"A sheep loses its way owing to a multiplicity of bypaths possible to take," Xindou Tzu expounded, "while a student that shows a plural doctrine fritters his life away. There is no marked difference in the source of all doctrines, but the bypaths lead to differed places. Only by returning to the ultimate source can one avoid going astray. Alas! You've followed Yang Tzu for a long time, studying his doctrine, and yet you don't get the hang of his moral representation."

——from *Lie Tzu*

Application

When in the presence of confused complexity, one is prone to be misled somewhere or reach nowhere on the condition that he is not rightly directed.

献鸠放生

邯郸之民以正月之旦献鸠于简子。简子大悦,厚赏之。

客问其故。简子曰:"正旦放生,示有恩也。"

客曰:"民知君之欲放之,故竞而捕之,死者众矣。君如欲生之,不若禁民勿捕。捕而放之,恩过不相补矣。"

简子曰:"然。"

——《列子》

警 言

人应多做好事,多做善事,但不应只讲形式,不讲究实际效果,或是假仁假义,沽名钓誉。出于真心的,做不成,也不必惭愧;出于作秀的,做成了,也未必积得了功德。善心和善举同样重要,但善举之下是否存在善心,我们应该学会辨别。

Catching Turtledoves for Grace Release

By convention the people of Handan captured turtledoves to present on Chinese New Year's Day to Jian Tzu, prince of the state of Zhao, who was always exhilarated at it and paid handsome rewards to them.

Questioned by his counsellor and follower why he had this convention practised, Jian Tzu claimed, "I have the captive turtledoves set free to bestow my grace."

Then came his counsellor's words, 'Knowing that you have the intention to let go captive turtledoves, your subjects vied to grab at the birds for you, to find a great many killed in the course of capture."

"Should you have a severe intent to let them sustain their lives, you had better prohibit people from taking animals captive for grace release," he continued. "With capture for that sake, your benevolence will not be able to suffice to be compensations for the atrocious consequence."

"Agreed," Jian Tzu responded, approvingly.

——from *Lie Tzu*

Application

It is noble of one to practise charity or beneficence. However, formalistic practice, with no veritable rewards brought to being, or hypocrisy for name and fame ought to be but undesired. Failed philanthropy out of severity brings forth no shame while pretensions in the name of charity that is impeccably done may not lead to recorded merit according to God's judgment. With kindness-deriving intention and meritorious acts of great import, whether or not it is a virtuous deed of well-meaning intention should come to a thorough understanding.

宋人拾契

宋人有游于道,得人遗契者,归而藏之,密数其齿。告邻人曰:"吾富可待矣。"

——《列子》

警言

财迷心窍的人,被眼前的财富蒙蔽了双眼,不能辨识财富的真实度,这是很可悲的。

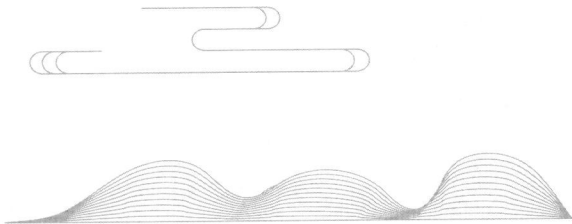

A Man Picking Up a Deed

A man of the state of Song was roaming the street where he came across a nullified title deed, along with which he made for his home. Hiding the deed somewhere, he counted the items on it in secret. "I am going to make a fortune," he bragged to a neighbour.

——from *Lie Tzu*

Application

He who is obsessed with the aspirations for money tends to have a missed look at whether or not it is veritable, which is a pathetic manner of practice.

枯梧不祥

人有枯梧树者,其邻父言枯梧之树不祥,其邻人遽而伐之。邻人父因请以为薪。其人乃不悦,曰:"邻人之父徒欲为薪而教吾伐之也。与我邻,若此其险,岂可哉?"

——《列子》

有的人提出意见或建议时,往往是出于个人的私利。因此,我们在面对他人给出的意见或建议时,要理智鉴别,不能盲从。

The Withered Phoenix Tree to Incur Bad Luck

There stood a phoenix tree in the yard of a man, whose neighbour, an old man, commented that keeping a withered phoenix tree incurred misfortune. Upon this, the man spared no time to fell the tree before the old neighbour called for some cut down twigs as firewood. The owner of the tree himself thereby became indignant. "That's why he offered me the advice to chop the tree. Living next door to me is so crafty a neighbour—that won't do," he concluded, gruntingly.

——from *Lie Tzu*

Application

With the suggestion-maker driven oftentimes by the profit likely to obtain, suggestions that are offered to you demand to be meticulously discerned. Therefore, it is senseless of you to act in blind compliance with the received suggestions.

失斧疑邻

人有亡斧者，意其邻之子。视其行步，窃斧也；颜色，窃斧也；言语，窃斧也；动作态度无为而不窃斧也。俄而抇其谷而得其斧，他日复见其邻之子，动作态度无似窃斧者。

——《列子》

警言

主观成见会影响人对事物的判断。对人对事，须避免主观臆断，方能进行谨慎客观的判断，从而抵达真相。

An Axe Lost, the Neighbour's Son to Suspect

A man who lost his axe suspected his neighbour's son of committing the theft. Scrutinizing the gait with which the lad walked, he assured himself of the young one stealing the axe. With the guy's countenance looked into, he was convinced that he was the thief. Furthermore, the young man's way of talking justified his suspicion from one more perspective. All in all, no actions or gestures do not contribute to a representation of the boy's being a thief.

Presently, the man found his axe while he was digging in the valley.

Some other day, he saw his neighbour's son, when none of the lad's actions or gestures looked the likes of a thief.

———from *Lie Tzu*

Application

A preconceived idea or impression on a person or happening can mislead one's judgment to be made. Faced with either someone or something, one should evade subjective assumption in an utmost attempt to conduct a meticulous, objective judgment to achieve the truth.

齐人攫金

昔齐人有欲金者。清旦衣冠而之市,适鬻金者之所,因攫其金而去。吏捕得之,问曰:"人皆在焉,子攫人之金何?"对曰:"取金之时,不见人,徒见金。"

——《列子》

警 言

若利欲熏心、见钱眼开,则极易被眼前的利益所蒙蔽而做出违背法律或道德的愚蠢行为。

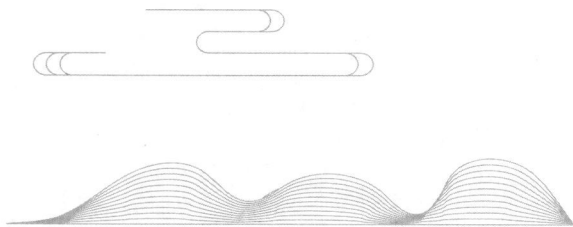

A Man Seizing Upon Gold

Once upon a time, there lived a man in the state of Qi who aspired to gold. One morning, putting on his coat and hat, he headed to the market, where coming to a gold-dealer's, he seized upon the dealer's gold and made off.

"How come you thieve gold in the presence of the throng?" the sheriff who caught him questioned.

"As I seize hold of the gold," he replied, "I cast my eyes upon no one but the gold."

——from *Lie Tzu*

Application

Once overdriven by momentary profit or one's eye captured by money, one tends to be blinded by the immediate favours in his presence, thereby throwing himself into unbecoming behaviours in violation of the law or morality.

斥鷃讥鹏

有鸟焉,其名为鹏,背若太山,翼若垂天之云。抟扶摇羊角而上者九万里,绝云气,负青天,然后图南,且适南冥也。斥鷃笑之曰:"彼且奚适也?我腾跃而上,不过数仞而下,翱翔蓬蒿之间,此亦飞之至也。而彼且奚适也?"此小大之辩也。

——《庄子》

如果人的眼界只在蓬蒿之间,那么眼里尽是障碍与束缚,会限制视野和高飞的动力。反之,若眼界能够指向开阔之地,则眼里尽是青天碧景,会扩大视野,增强了飞远、飞高的愿望。

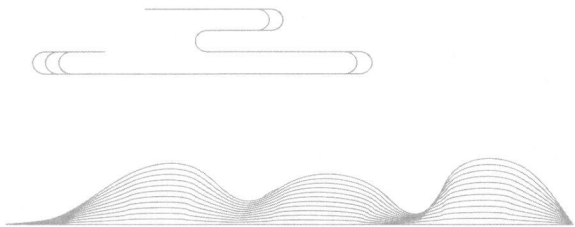

The Titmouse and the Roc

There was once a giant bird called the roc, whose back rose as high as Mount Tai and whose wings overspread the heavens as wide as clouds. The roc rocketed up over ninety thousand *li* in a whirl of air, soaring through the misty vapours against the azure sky. On southward flight, he headed to the South Sea.

"Where can the roc be going?" scoffed a titmouse. "I leap up to scores of feet among the shrubs at the extremity of the height I can possibly reach. Where can he go?"

Therein lies the differentiation between great and small, of which the roc and the titmouse respectively are representative.

——from *Zhuang Tzu*

Application

When one's eye falls amid thickets, one has all obstacles and constraints in sight, which limits his horizons, impeding him from soaring. On the contrary, once his eye gets at a greater expanse of space, his sight is a container of the blue skies, thereby his horizons broadered, which enhances his aspirations to clear his way to an overwhelming height.

不龟手之药

宋人有善为不龟手之药者，世世以洴澼絖为事。客闻之，请买其方百金。聚族而谋曰："我世世为洴澼絖，不过数金；今一朝而鬻技百金，请与之。"客得之，以说吴王。越有难，吴王使之将。冬，与越人水战，大败越人，裂地而封之。能不龟手一也，或以封，或不免于洴澼絖，则所用之异也。

——《庄子》

警 言

这个故事告诉我们，同一事物其价值和效用可大可小，大小完全是把握在人对资源的利用上的。资源利用的角度不同，导致事物的价值和效用不同。

The Ointment for Chapped Hands

A family of the state of Song who could produce ointment for chapped hands engaged in laundering from generation to generation. A man who was told of this offered a hundred taels of gold for the recipe, which called the whole house to a meeting for discussion. "We've been in the laundering trade for generations," said the family, "with income adding up to no more than several taels of gold. However, we earn a hundred pieces of gold by giving away our recipe. Let's sell it anyway." Now the state of Yue waged a war against the state of Wu. With the recipe, the man presented King of Wu, who then appointed the recipe offerer as general. That winter, the Wu troops engaged the enemy on the river, overcoming those of Yue, the man awarded a fief. The use to which the same ointment recipe for chapped hands is put leads to different access, either to possession of a fief or hand relief in the process of laundering.

——from *Zhuang Tzu*

Application

This fable shows the value of the same thing may stretch from great to little, depending on the use to which the thing is put. The difference between the ways in which the thing comes into use leads to the difference in its value and utility.

庄周梦蝶

昔者庄周梦为蝴蝶，栩栩然胡蝶也。自喻适志与，不知周也。俄然觉，则蘧蘧然周也。不知周之梦为胡蝶与，胡蝶之梦为周与？周与胡蝶，则必有分矣。此之谓物化。

——《庄子》

警言

人生中，有时梦境和现实是很难区分的。梦境可能给人真实的感觉，而真实的人生也可能给人梦境的不真实感。在梦境中与蝴蝶化为一体，轻快飞舞，实现了其灵魂的自由。要坚守内心，不要被世俗羁绊，不为形役，不为物累，拥有自由的灵魂。

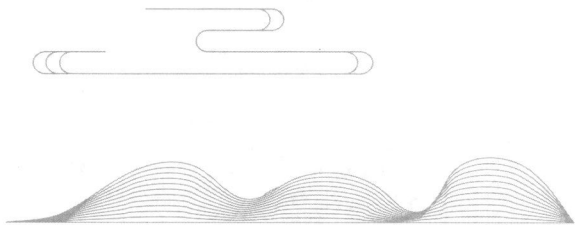

Zhuang Tzu Coming
in the Form of a Butterfly in His Dream

Zhuang Zhou, in his dream, converted into a butterfly that was fluttering briskly and freely, unaware of itself being Zhuang Zhou with much elation. Of a sudden, he awoke from his sleep, coming to the sense that he was Zhou rather than a butterfly. It remains unknown whether Zhou had a dream in which he changed into a butterfly or the butterfly had a dream in which it turned into Zhou. Zhou and the butterfly, who came in varied forms, must be physically distinguished from one another in the earthly eye, which is termed reification.

——from *Zhuang Tzu*

Application

On some occasions, it is unintelligible of a marked distinction between the insubstantial dream and the actual reality. The dream may transport you to a realistic world which, in turn, presumably brings you to a solid feel of an illusionary reality. Fluttering up and down in the form of the butterfly in the dream, Zhuang Zhou set free his soul. Cleave to your aspirations, refraining from material constraints, and you will be in possession of the unshackled spirit.

臧榖亡羊

臧与榖，二人相与牧羊而俱亡其羊。问臧奚事，则挟策读书；问榖奚事，则博塞以游。二人者，事业不同，其于亡羊均也。

——《庄子》

警言

坏的结果，无论具体原因是什么，本质都没有差别，均是导致了恶果的因。不管工作时是读书，还是玩耍，玩忽职守不负责任，本质上都是一种不敬职、不敬业的行为，都是错的。

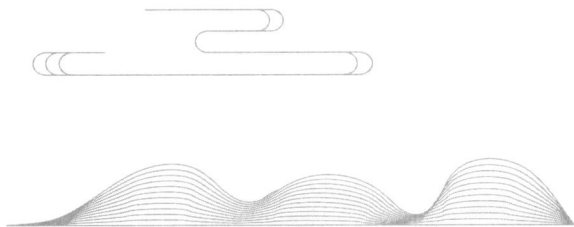

中国寓言故事选英译

Two Shepherds' Loss of Sheep

Two boys, Zang and Gu, went shepherding together, both of whom lost their sheep. Questioned what he had been engaged in, Zang said that he busied himself with reading. When asked what he had been up to, Gu replied that he had been playing draughts.

Differently occupied as they were, the two boy shepherds' flocks herding stories shared the same ending.

——from *Zhuang Tzu*

Application

No matter how different they appear, the occurrences that have brought the undesirable consequence are taken as the same in nature. Negligence at work with lack of sense of duty, in essence, is a practice with little commitment to one's job in spite of what the focus you have laid on, a noble deed such as reading or simply playing. It is unacceptably wrong of you to engage yourself in whatever else grabs your attention from your assigned commitment.

东施效颦

西施病心而矉其里，其里之丑人见而美之，归亦捧心而矉其里。其里之富人见之，坚闭门而不出；贫人见之，挈妻子而去之走。彼知矉美，而不知矉之所以美。

——《庄子》

警 言

不根据自己的特点而盲目地模仿，结果可能适得其反。在提升自己形象的过程中，需考虑自身的具体特点，根据特点进行改变，扬长避短，寻找适合自己的形象。盲目模仿是愚蠢的。在个人发展的过程中，同样需要考虑自身的具体情况，盲目地照搬照抄可能导致失败的结果。

The Ugly Girl's Imitated Frown

Xi Shi, the noted belle, suffered from a heart disease, which gave rise to her frequent frown, with even more beauty added to her comely face.

An ugly girl, who lived in the same village, noticed Xi Shi's stunning beauty during her heart attack. She thereupon frowned, her hands laid to her breast. The rich, when they chanced to meet her, barred their doors, refusing to come out, and the poor took to their heels with their wives and children.

She was aware of the beauty presented in Xi Shi's frown, which she failed to justify to her confused self.

——from *Zhuang Tzu*

Application

With specified conditions ignored, methods adopted in imitation of someone else can presumably lead to a reversed ending. To raise your image to a betterment, should your specific characteristics be weighed, favourable alterations made, and strengths fully developed, you would be able to make your ideal visualization materialize. Admittedly, it is unbecoming of you to be a complete copy of a better one than yourself. Likewise, in terms of your personal growth, measurement of down-to-earth conditions is vital for any blind imitation with no essential adaptations may conduct you to failure.

埳井之蛙

埳井之鼃谓东海之鳖曰："吾乐与！出跳梁乎井幹之上，入休乎缺甃之崖；赴水则接腋持颐，蹶泥则没足灭跗；还虷、蟹与科斗，莫吾能若也。且夫擅一壑之水，而跨跱埳井之乐，此亦至矣。夫子奚不时来入观乎？"东海之鳖左足未入，而右膝已絷矣。于是逡巡而却，告之海曰："夫千里之远，不足以举其大；千仞之高，不足以极其深。禹之时十年九潦，而水弗为加益；汤之时八年七旱，而崖不为加损。夫不为顷久推移，不以多少进退者，此亦东海之大乐也。"于是埳井之鼃闻之，适适然惊，规规然自失也。

——《庄子》

警 言

目光短浅的人永远走不出自己的小世界，眼光总是局限于自己所处的环境，要把眼光放得长远些，多看看外面的世界。世界无限广阔，知识永无穷尽，无论处世还是求学，我们都应虚心，不断接触新世界、新事物，不断增长见识、充实自己。

The Frog in the Well

"How beatific I am here!" a frog living in a shallow well bragged to a big turtle from the East Sea, "I can scamper along the edge of the well mouth when I'm out and rest in the crevice of the wall of the well. I can wallow in the water which props up my head and forearms to my heart's content, or step ankle deep in the mud and muck. Looking around, I dare say no wigglers or crabs or tadpoles can compare with me. I have the water world in the well all to myself. The delight I take in being lord of this shallow well is the acme of happiness that a fellow can possibly obtain. Why not come down in the well to pay me a visit more often?"

Hardly had the turtle had his left claw into the well when his right knee got caught on the edge of the mouth of the well, which brought him to a momentary halt and a fruitless retreat. Upon this, he then pictured the sea to the frog. "A thousand leagues does not suffice for an accurate account of how broad the sea is and a thousand feet does not suffice for that of how deep it is. During the reign of Yu, the founding emperor of the Xia Dynasty, with floods in nine years out of every ten, the deep never rises in the slightest degree. In the reign of Tang, the founding emperor of the Shang Dynasty, when droughts frequented the country as often as in seven years every eight, the ocean water was not found less. It is the uttermost joy for the sea to retain a constant amount of water throughout the ages." Struck by the turtle's words, the frog went ashamed and abashed.

——from *Zhuang Tzu*

Application

If short-sighted, you are prone to fail to struggle out of your limited world, with your eyes laid on circumscribed life. Stretch your vision to somewhere beyond what surrounds you, and you will drag yourself to a bigger, broader world where you may have an improved knowledge of yourself and the heightened value of life. Knowledge goes as infinite as the world can be. Therefore, in terms of how to be a social being or an academic figure, we should retain a modest heart, keeping ourselves updated with new ideas, concepts or skills.

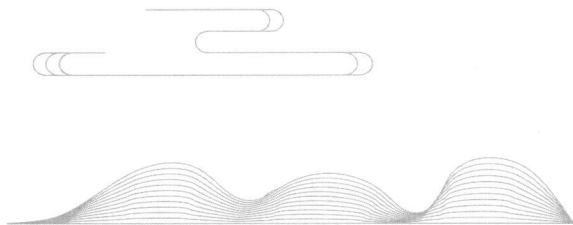

邯郸学步

且子不闻夫寿陵馀子之学行于邯郸与？未得国能，又失其故行矣，直匍匐而归耳。

——《庄子》

警 言

盲目崇拜并模仿，生搬硬套，会失去自身本来的特色和优势，最终将适得其反，表现得不伦不类。不如做自己，保持自信，做一个独特的个体。

Learning to Walk with the Gait Practised in Handan

Have you heard the story of a young lad from Shouling learning to walk with the gait of those from Handan? Not only did he fail to have mastery of Handan people's unique walking skills, but his original walking gait got off his mind, which reduced him to his crawling back to the state of Yan.

——from *Zhuang Tzu*

Application

Blind worship and imitation may lead to the loss of one's own uniqueness or power, which may bring about an end that runs counter to one's desire, making him behave awkwardly.

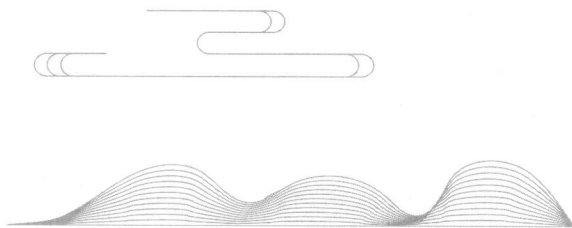

鲁侯养鸟

昔者海鸟止于鲁郊，鲁侯御而觞之于庙，奏《九韶》以为乐，具太牢以为膳。鸟乃眩视忧悲，不敢食一脔，不敢饮一杯，三日而死。此以己养养鸟也，非以鸟养养鸟也。

——《庄子》

警言

好的愿望须符合客观需求。倘若忽视了事物的客观规律，即便是出于善意，也可能导致不好的后果。为人处世切忌忽略人与人之间的差异，你认为好的，别人可能觉得是不好的。因此，如果将个人喜好强加于他人，往往会好心办了坏事。

The Marquis Keeping the Bird

A sea bird alighted somewhere in the suburban state of Lu, in which the marquis of the state took much delight. He received it with a feast of ancient music and supreme sacrifices in the ancestor temple, which startled it to a state of terrified bewilderment. This rendered the bird giddy and distressed, which was too frightened to take in a morsel of meat or a single cup of wine. It was only three days later that the bird went dead. It was an entertainment practised upon the Marquis himself that was practised upon the sea bird, as is to the man's liking rather than to the bird.

——from *Zhuang Tzu*

Application

Good intentions should conform to objective demands, regardless of which, any severe kindness can presumably conduce to undesirable results. As a social being, you do avoid neglecting the difference between people, that is to say, what you believe best may not be interpreted as the same. Therefore, should aspirations of your own be imposed upon someone else, the chance of bad consequences could scarcely be slim.

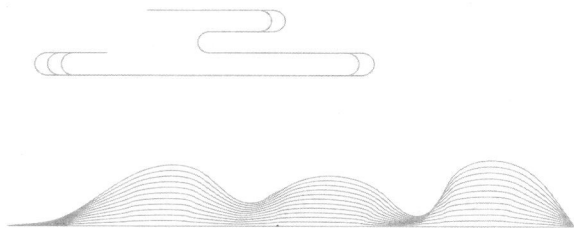

捉蝉的学问

仲尼适楚，出于林中，见痀偻者承蜩，犹掇之也。仲尼曰："子巧乎！有道邪？"曰："我有道也。五六月累丸二而不坠，则失者锱铢；累三而不坠，则失者十一；累五而不坠，犹掇之也。吾处身也，若厥株拘；吾执臂也，若槁木之枝。虽天地之大，万物之多，而唯蜩翼之知。吾不反不侧，不以万物易蜩之翼，何为而不得！"孔子顾谓弟子曰："用志不分，乃凝于神，其痀偻丈人之谓乎！"

——《庄子》

警 言

做事须专心致志，勤学苦练，讲求方法，坚持不懈。这不仅仅适用于捉蝉，也适用于学习和工作。

On How to Catch the Cicada

On the way to the state of Chu, Confucius, along with his students, went in a wood for a rest. As they came out of the wood, he saw an old hunchbacked man catching cicadas with a pole of bamboo. He employed the pole to the degree of dexterity that he missed not a single cicada as if he were catching with his own hands.

"How adept you are! Are there some tips?" marvelled Confucius.

"Yes, there are. With two projectiles stacked up on one end of pole, practise holding the pole five to six months until they wouldn't come off," responded the hunchback. "Then, fewer misses would occur."

"Provided that with three projectiles stacked on one end of pole, I could manipulate the pole," he explained further, "then I was able to have one miss out of ten attempts."

"When five projectiles piled up one by one on one end of pole, I could take control of the pole without any projectile falling off," he continued, "I wouldn't have one single miss as if I were catching cicadas with my hands."

"I stand myself to be as still as a stump can be," he added. "I hold the bamboo pole with my arm to make it feel nothing but a sere branch. Despite there being the broad skies and earth and a multitude of things between them, my attention is focused just on the cicada wings."

"As I keep every part of my body still, my focus not taken by the numerous distractions off the cicadas, why can't I catch the insects?" concluded the old man, wise.

On hearing these words, Confucius turned around to his students. "Concentration or focus is what the hunchbacked old man has suggested," he said.

——from *Zhuang Tzu*

Application

No matter what it is — catching cicadas, studies or work, concentration, diligent practice, resort to the right methodology and methods, and endurance are required for a good job.

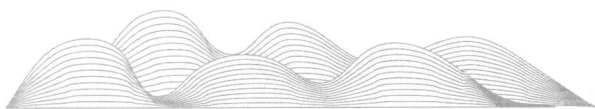

中国寓言故事选英译

呆若木鸡

纪渻子为王养斗鸡。十日而问:"鸡已乎?"曰:"未也。方虚憍而恃气。"十日又问,曰:"未也。犹应向景。"十日又问,曰:"未也。犹疾视而盛气。"十日又问,曰:"几矣。鸡虽有鸣者,已无变矣,望之似木鸡矣,其德全矣,异鸡无敢应者,反走矣。"

——《庄子》

警言

有些品行未必天生使然,积习成性罢了。

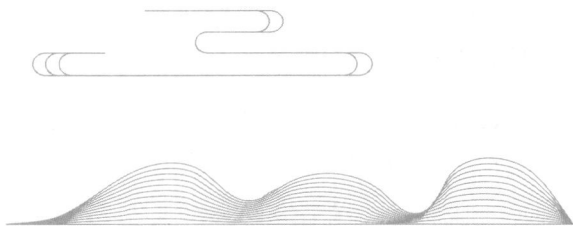

As Stupefied as a Wooden Cock

Ten days after Ji Sheng Tzu was given a cock to keep for cockfighting, he was enquired whether the cock was able to fight.

"Not yet. The cock's bearing remains of restlessness, haughtiness and insolence," the cock raiser and trainer replied.

Another ten days went by before he was summoned for the same question again.

"Not yet. With other cocks to the ear or to the eye, the cock got into immediate reactions," as his reply went.

As ten more days passed, the man was questioned another time.

"Not yet. The cock is still subject to fleeting glances and bellicose disposition," responded the cock trainer.

With the passage of another ten days, the man was bid to give the answer to the same question.

"Almost done. Pugnacious as other cocks are with crows upon crows let out, this cock was not stimulated to even a stir, looking a wooden cock, which has been equipped with all natural qualities as a fighting cock. Unafraid of coming to meet this opponent, other cocks tend to turn tail when this stupefied-looking cock jumps in their sight."

——from *Zhuang Tzu*

Application

Some conducts or bearings do not come by nature, but they are developed through long-period training.

匠石运斤

庄子送葬,过惠子之墓,顾谓从者曰:"郢人垩慢其鼻端,若蝇翼,使匠石斫之。匠石运斤成风,听而斫之,尽垩而鼻不伤,郢人立不失容。宋元君闻之,召匠石曰:'尝试为寡人为之。'匠石曰:'臣则尝能斫之。虽然,臣之质死久矣。'自夫子之死也,吾无以为质矣,吾无与言之矣。"

——《庄子》

警 言

精湛超群的技艺,其力量往往超过缺少智慧的力气。真正欣赏超群技艺的人并信任其技艺者可谓知音。千金易得,知音难求。

Stone a Craftsman Manipulating the Axe

On his way to a burial ceremony, Zhuang Tzu passed by the tomb of Hui Tzu. Therewith he turned to his entourage and said, "There lived a man in Ying, capital of Chu, who whitewashed houses for a living. Once he found a tiny speck of slurry on the tip of his nose, which was as thin as the wing of the fly. He then asked Stone a Craftsman to get it off his nose tip. Stone swung an axe at the nose, letting out a whir, the stain completely removed and the nose intact. As he was waiting to be deprived of the slurry mark, the whitewasher stood still, his complexion unchanged. Informed of this, King Yuan of Song sent for the craftsman and let him chop off the like spot on his nose tip. Yet the man refused. 'I used to be able to do that,' he explained. 'Even if I can do that now, I insist not because the one to whom my skill can be carried out is gone.' Since Hui Tzu passed away, there has been none to debate with."

——from *Zhuang Tzu*

Application

The power of extraordinary skills is ten times that of one's physical strength. Those who appreciate this power of extraordinary skills and may entrust one's life to it are rare. A thousand taels of gold is easy to obtain while a real friend appreciative of one's talent is hard to get.

吴王射猴

吴王浮于江,登乎狙之山,众狙见之,恂然弃而走,逃于深蓁。有一狙焉,委蛇攫抓,见巧乎王。王射之,敏给搏捷矢。王命相者趋射之,狙执死。

——《庄子》

警 言

这则寓言告诉我们,不论一个人有多高的技能或智慧,都不应该在他人面前炫耀,更不应轻视他人。过分炫耀和自大、拿别人当傻子,会招致不必要的麻烦,甚至导致灾难性的后果。有自知之明、谦虚谨慎才是为人处世之道。

The King Shooting the Monkey

As the king of the state of Wu came to the mountain that monkeys inhabited after crossing the Yangtze River, a gathering of monkeys, panic-stricken, scattered about into the depth of the thorns and shrubberies except one of them. This monkey leapt a leisurely leap up and down with conceited elation, showing its art and techniques. Seeing this, the king pulled his bow and let go an arrow toward the primate, who nimbly caught hold of the fleeting arrow. Then the king made an order that his archers release arrows quickly, which shot at the monkey in number greater than that it could attend to. Therefore, the monkey was shot dead.

——from *Zhuang Tzu*

Application

The fable warns us that despite one's great capability, one ought not to make a show of it or slight others' power or ability due to his own fantastic techniques. A show of oneself, conceit or belittling others may incur unnecessary trouble, leading to a disastrous consequence. Meticulous modesty is a widely-accepted philosophy of life.

涸辙之鲋

庄周家贫，故往贷粟于监河侯。监河侯曰："诺。我将得邑金，将贷子三百金，可乎？"

庄周忿然作色曰："周昨来，有中道而呼者。周顾视车辙中，有鲋鱼焉。周问之曰：'鲋鱼来！子何为者邪？'对曰：'我，东海之波臣也。君岂有斗升之水而活我哉？'周曰："诺。我且南游吴越之王，激西江之水而迎子，可乎？'鲋鱼忿然作色曰：'吾失我常与，我无所处。吾得斗升之水然活耳。君乃言此，曾不如早索我于枯鱼之肆！'"

——《庄子》

警言

漂亮的诺言往往很难兑现。应许漂亮的诺言，是不愿意去解决实际问题的常用伎俩。庄子用自己对鲋许下的承诺以讽刺监河侯不办实事、不帮助他解决实际困难。

The Carp in the Dry Rut

Zhuang Zhou, who was money-deprived, went to the Lord Keeper of the River for a loan of grains.

"Fine," said the lord. "I shall presently collect the taxes from my fiefdom. And then I'm going to give you a loan of gold of three hundred taels, ain't I?"

Indignant, Zhuang Zhou told him, "While I was on my way here yesterday I was called by someone. As I looked around, I found it was a carp trapped in a dry rut on the road.

"'How come did you get there, Carp?' I asked.

"'I lived in the East Sea,' he replied. 'Could you please get a barrel of water to save my life?'

"'That's all right. Since I'm going south for a visit to pay to the kings of the two states of Wu and Yue,' I promised, 'I shall request them to let through water from the West River to the here, shan't I?'

"Upon these words of mine, the carp was struck with indignation. 'I am out of my natural element, without which there is no chance for me to survive,' he complained. 'Only with a barrel of water would I be saved. You'd rather seek me in the dried fish market than make so empty a promise.'"

——from *Zhuang Tzu*

Application

A void promise can hardly be kept, referred to as a usual trick not to settle the existing problem. Through the tale spinned with a carp in the dry rut, Zhuang Tzu proposes a sarcastic comment on those who attempt to avoid settling a trouble by practical means but resort to giving an empty offer hardly to be achieved.

屠龙之技

朱泙漫学屠龙于支离益，单千金之家。三年技成而无所用其巧。

——《庄子》

警 言

这则寓言告诉我们，在学习和工作中，须从实际出发，讲求实际效果。若脱离了对实际所能达成效果的考量，再大的本领也没有意义。

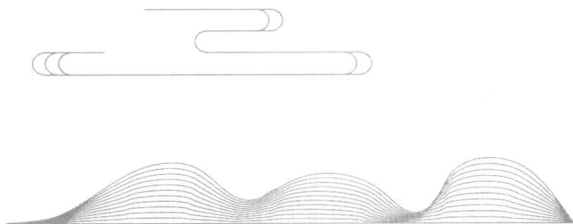

The Art of Slaying Dragons

Zhu Pingman learnt to slay dragons from Zhili Yi for three years long, all his wealth of gold expended on his mastery of the skill, only to find his acquired skill had occasion to be applied nowhere.

——from *Zhuang Tzu*

Application

This fable is so true a picture of the divorce between practice and what one has learnt. The target skill to acquire, deviating from pragmatic route, is destined to bring him to nothingness.

五十步笑百步

梁惠王曰:"寡人之于国也,尽心焉耳矣。河内凶,则移其民于河东,移其粟于河内。河东凶亦然。察邻国之政,无知寡人之用心者,邻国之民不加少,寡人之民不加多,何也?"

孟子对曰:"王好战,请以战喻。填然鼓之,兵刃既接,弃甲曳兵而走,或百步而后止,或五十步而后止。以五十步笑百步,则何如?"

曰:"不可。直不百步耳,是亦走也。"

——《孟子》

警 言

自己跟他人犯了同样的错误或有同样的缺点,只是程度上轻一些,却去嘲笑他人的程度略重些的缺点,这样的做法忽略了自身与他人均有错误的本质。透过现象看到本质,方能更好地发现问题,以实现从本质上纠正自身错误的目的。

The Less Mistaken Laughing
at the More Mistaken

"For the sake of the state, I have exerted all my energies," King Hui of the state of Wei argued. "As north of the Yellow River prevailed famine due to crop failures, I moved the people east and had millet grains transported to the north of the Yellow River for relief. So did I when famine occurred to the east of the River. Those rulers of the neighbouring states looked into, none attend to the people so much as I do. However, their populations are found on the decrease and mine is not seen increasing. Why is that?"

"Now that Your Majesty has a tendency for engagement," Mencius responded, "please let me exemplify my point with a war-related phenomenon. Once the war drums sound, arms crossed in the air, the troops engage the enemy until the defeated abandon their armour and flee trailing their weapons behind them. Some of them retreat a hundred yards while others fifty before they stop going backward. Is it becoming for those who run back fifty yards to laugh at those who retreat a hundred?"

"Of course not," commented King Hui. "They run back less than a hundred yards, but they turn tail the same way."

——from *Mencius*

Application

Making a mistake to a smaller degree, one feels like that he has the advantage of scoffing at those whose mistake is identified as bigger. This practice roots from the ignorance of the fact that mistakes, small or big, hold the nature of no difference. Therefore, see the quintessence through what's on the face to locate where the issue lies in a bid to right a wrong in the true sense of the meaning.

以羊易牛

王坐于堂上，有牵牛而过堂下者，王见之，曰："牛何之？"对曰："将以衅钟。"王曰："舍之！吾不忍其觳觫，若无罪而就死地。"对曰："然则废衅钟与？"曰："何可废也？以羊易之。"

——《孟子》

警 言

无论是杀牛还是杀羊本质上都是残忍的，以羊易牛只是掩饰残忍的虚伪仁慈。

中国寓言故事选英译

A Sheep in Place of an Ox

As the king of the state of Qi was sitting at the palace, someone led an ox past the hall. At the sight of this, the king enquired, "Where is the ox led?"

"To the bell as an offering," replied the man.

"Let it go. I can't bear to see that it's looking terrified, waiting to be slaughtered in spite of its being guiltless,' suggested the king.

"In this case, will the sacrifice be abolished then?" wondered the man.

"Why do away with the sacrifice? Replace the ox with a sheep," proposed the one on the throne.

——from *Mencius*

Application

The killing of an ox or a sheep for sacrifice, in the true sense of the meaning, is a cruel, savage and barbaric practice. To substitute a sheep for an ox is pretended mercy with cruelty in disguise.

拔苗助长

宋人有闵其苗不长而揠之者，芒芒然归，谓其人曰："今日病矣，予助苗长矣。"其子趋而往视之，苗则槁矣。天下之不助苗长者寡矣。以为无益而舍之者，不耕苗者也。助之长者，揠苗者也，非徒无益，而又害之。

——《孟子》

警 言

任何事物都有其自身的发展规律，遵循事物之发展规律能够事半功倍；若违反之，仅凭借一腔热情和美好的愿望，急于求成，则将事倍功半。

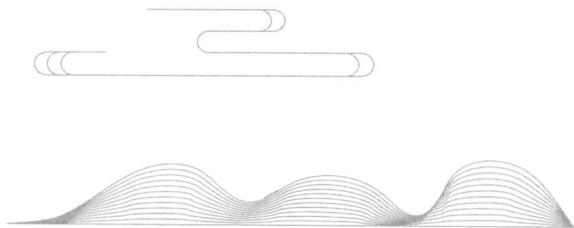

Pulling Up Seedlings for Their Growth

In the state of Song lived a man, who was somehow afraid that the seedlings in his fields were not growing, which brought him to a decision to tug them upward one by one. Then, he went home, exhausted, and said to his family, "I'm worn out today. I pulled up rows upon rows of seedlings to let them grow faster." His son made a haste down to the fields for a check, only to find all the shoots withered. Those who fail to hasten the seedlings' growth are few. Some regard their toil as meaningless, even making no attempt to weed the fields at all. Others who struggle to assist the shoots in their growth tug them upward, to which not good but harm is done.

———from *Mencius*

Application

Every single subject develops in compliance with a certain law. Conform to it, and you will be able to be twice fruitful with half your toil; run counter to it, eager for the fruit with merely a burst of enthusiasm and earnest aspirations, and you are bound to labour painstakingly but to little avail.

楚人学齐语

孟子谓戴不胜曰："子欲子之王之善与？我明告子。有楚大夫于此，欲其子之齐语也，则使齐人傅诸，使楚人傅诸？"

曰："使齐人傅之。"

曰："一齐人傅之，众楚人咻之，虽日挞而求其齐也，不可得矣；引而置之庄岳之间数年，虽日挞而求其楚，亦不可得矣。子谓薛居州善士也，使之居于王所。在于王所者，长幼卑尊皆薛居州也，王谁与为不善？在王所者，长幼卑尊皆非薛居州也，王谁与为善？一薛居州，独如宋王何？"

——《孟子》

警言

橘生淮南则为橘，生于淮北则为枳。环境对人的影响极大，人总是会自然而然地适应所生存的自然或人文环境。人的语言、习俗、习惯、品德和修养等均受到周围环境的影响。

A Boy from Chu to Learn
the Language of Qi

Mencius said to Dai Busheng, a minister of the state of Song, "Do you feel like His Majesty is inclined to good turns? Let me tell you something. Given that a senior official of Chu wants his son to speak the language of Qi, which, do you think, is better, to get a teacher from Qi or from Chu to teach him?"

"I think it better to learn under a teacher from Qi," Dai Busheng smiled, quite assured.

"Well, a teacher speaks to him the language of Qi while in the meantime a multitude of men from Chu make an awful din. In this circumstance, even if he is compelled by means of daily flogging or lashing to use the language, he can't manage to do that. If he is let live in a most populous town of Qi for some years, even flogged or lashed each day, he won't be liable to speak Chu's language," asserted Mencius.

"As you said, Xue Juzhou is a man of virtue and credit. Let him live around His Majesty," continued Mencius. "On condition that those who live in the palace, whether old or young, superior or inferior, are without exception of his kind, with whom the king can be up to no good?"

"On the contrary, if those who surround the ruler, no matter what category they are of, are not of the like kind, with whom the king can do good?" argued Mencius. "With only one man of good quality around, how can the king succumb to this very inclination for virtue?"

——from *Mencius*

Application

The element decides the orange to be edible and sweet or to be inedible and bitter. The environment, in which the language, customs, habits, virtue and moral cultivation are fostered and develop, has a huge influence on men who are most likely to adapt naturally to what exists as the sustaining necessity.

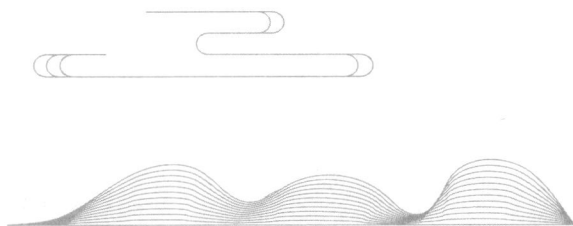

攘邻之鸡

今有人日攘其邻之鸡者,或告之曰:"是非君子之道。"曰:"请损之,月攘一鸡,以待来年,然后已。"如知其非义,斯速已矣,何待来年?

——《孟子》

警 言

一旦做了错事,若得知其为锴,则须改正错误,而不能满足于错误数量的减少。否则,虽然减少了错误的存在,并未改变错误的本质。

The Chicken Thief

Now there was a man who thieved a chicken from his neighbours daily.

"Theft goes against the doctrine of a gentleman," someone said to him.

"Please allow me to cut down on theft," he responded beggingly, "by stealing one chicken monthly. It is next year that I'm going to completely quit stealing."

Aware of the immorality, he ought to have brought the misconduct to an end. Why wait until the ensuing year?

——from *Mencius*

Application

Aware of misconduct, one ought to call for it to cease rather than pursuing a decrease in it. Otherwise, reduced misconduct remains what it is, which changed its nature of theft in vain.

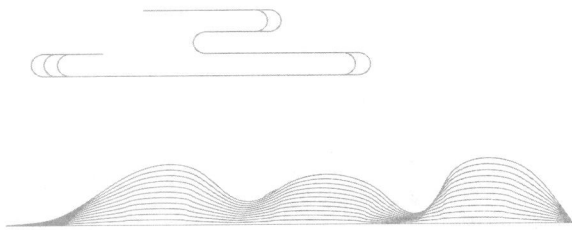

弈秋诲弈

弈之为数，小数也；不专心致志，则不得也。弈秋，通国之善弈者也。使弈秋诲两人弈，其一人专心致志，惟弈秋之为听。一人虽听之，一心以为有鸿鹄将至，思援弓缴而射之，虽与之俱学，弗若之矣。为是其智弗若与？曰："非然也。"

——《孟子》

警言

学习做事须专心致志，不可三心二意。不同的学习态度与专注程度，可能导致学习效果截然不同，决定学习效果的往往不是智力。

Two Student Players
Under the Same Teacher

As one of the arts, playing draughts is considered to be a minor one. In spite of this, you cannot acquire it without your devoted commitment paid to the learning process. Player Qiu, whose name was Qiu and was called so owing to his extraordinary art in playing draughts, recognized as the best draughts-player, was let teach two students to play. One of the two was wholly committed to what Player Qiu taught while the other, both ears seemingly open to the teacher, had his mind on the wild geese to fly past, itching for his bow and arrows with which to shoot them. Under the same mentor as they learnt, the latter one was not as excellent a student as the former one. Was it because of the difference in intelligence? I argue, it's not.

——from *Mencius*

Application

Whole-heartedness required, commitment is the most valued quality in terms of learning or going on a mission. The difference in attitude toward learning and the degree of devotion contributes to the discrepancy in learning effect, which for the most part is led to not by intelligence quotient but by one's sharpened focus.

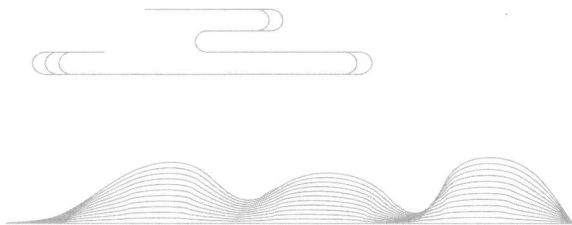

涓蜀梁疑鬼

夏首之南有人焉，曰涓蜀梁。其为人也，愚而善畏。明月而霄行，俯见其影，以为伏鬼也。卬视其发，以为立魅也，背而走，比至其家，失气而死。

——《荀子》

警 言

这个故事提醒我们，在面对生活中的各种问题时，应保持冷静和理智，勇于探查真相，避免因过度疑虑而造成心理和身体上的伤害。

A Man Scared of His Shadow

South of the Xia River Estuary lived a man, named Juan Shuliang, who was of slow wit and cowardice. One moonlit night, as he was walking, he happened to look down, his own shadow in sight, which he thought was a crouching ghost. Turning his head back up, with his dangling hair in the front into view, he thought the strand of hair to be the ghost to his feet. He thereby turned around in terror and shambled in panic on his way home. No sooner had he stepped into his home than he breathed his last.

——from *Xun Tzu*

Application

This fable warns us to retain our composure and senses in the face of startling events, to dig out the truth for the settlement of the issues, and not to consume so considerable a time and much energy for misgivings to the detriment of our physique and mind.

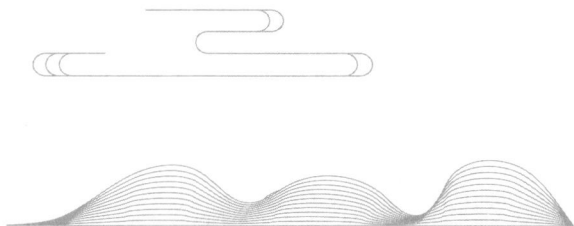

浮阳之鱼

鲦鲢者，浮阳之鱼也，胠于沙而思水，则无逮矣。挂于患而欲谨，则无益矣。自知者不怨人，知命者不怨天，怨人者穷，怨天者无志。失之己，反之人，岂不迂乎哉！

——《荀子》

不要到走上了绝路才想到要谨慎从事。要用发展的眼光估计客观情况的变化，能够自知并了解自然规律，从而防患于未然。不要做事后诸葛亮，更不要怨天尤人。

The Fish Bathing Themselves in the Sun

Such species of fish as Tiao and Qiao tend to stay outside of the water, bathing themselves in the sun. Once they are stranded at the beach, there will be no time that suffices for the fish to return to the water. Caught up in a calamity, the fish would find any after circumspection coming to no use at all. Those who can have a clear estimation of themselves never lay blame on any other party, those aware of their destiny not chastising the Heaven. The former ones are led into embarrassed adversity, the latter ones brought to short sight. When one errs, he in turn rebukes someone else. Isn't he going too far!

——from *Xun Tzu*

Application

Circumspection, which ought to be called to mind before adversity actually occurs, is of little consequence when you have come to a dead end. Any event or affair that is undergoing either positive or negative advances should be to the knowledge of one who can have a good understanding of both oneself and the nature's law, which may lead to prevention of vice from happening.

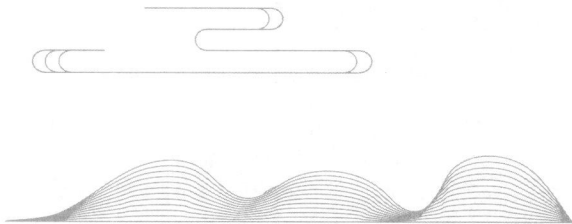

智子疑邻

宋有富人,大雨坏墙。其子曰"不筑,必将有盗。"其邻人之父亦云。暮而果大亡其财。其家甚智之子,而疑邻人之父。

——《韩非子》

警言

听取意见要选择正确的,而不要看重提意见的人与自己的关系。与自己关系亲密的未必能够提供正确的建议,而没有亲密关系的人提出的意见也不一定是有害的。因此,为人处世,要用心看问题,学会分析利弊,而不是偏听偏信。

Son Commended and Neighbour Suspected

In the state of Song lived a well-off man, whose wall went broken after a downpour of rain. "If you don't mend the wall," warned his son, "the opening is vulnerable to theft." An old neighbour of his made the same suggestion. That very night, he lost a big fortune, as both his son and the old neighbour predicted. The whole house of the rich man commended his son on his foresight while they suspected the old man of having committed the theft.

——from *Han Fei Tzu*

Application

When taking advice, you should make a wise judgment based not on how close you are to the advice-giver but on the applicability of the suggestion provided for you. In many circumstances, intimacy may not contribute to the correctness of the advice while those who do not have immediate relations may not bring forward misleading suggestions. Therefore, to be a social being, weigh pros and cons in your mind, avoiding biased reception of ideas.

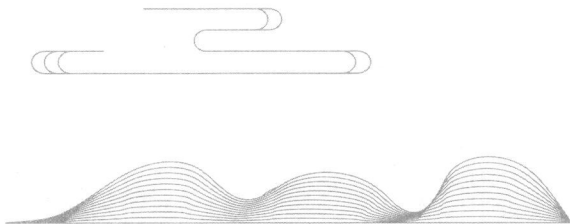

心不在马

赵襄主学御于王子于期，俄而与于期逐，三易马而三后。襄主曰："子之教我御，术未尽也？"对曰："术已尽，用之则过也。凡御之所贵：马体安于车，人心调于马，而后可以进速致远。今君后则欲逮臣，先则恐逮于臣。夫诱道争远，非先则后也，而先后心皆在于臣，上何以调于马？此君之所以后也。"

——《韩非子》

警言

得失计于心，则分心而不能集中精力。无论做任何事，专心致志比计较得失更易让人取得成就。

No Attention to the Horses

Zhao Xiang Tzu, king of the state of Zhao, learnt to drive a carriage under the tutelage of Wangzi Yuqi, a well-recognized carriage driver. It was not long before the king got to master the driving skills that the king asked the skillful driver to a carriage-driving race, in which he would like to race against his advisor. For the duration of the race, the learner exchanged his horses for his advisor's three times, to be found lost in three sessions of the race.

"Are there still skills you missed teaching me to drive?" questioned Zhao Xiang Tzu.

"No, sir. You have learnt all skills required to control the horse along with the carriage," the skilled carriage driver replied. "However, you haven't practised the skills proficiently on the horse and the carriage."

"What should be attended to while driving a carriage is that with the horses secured to the carriage, the driver's focus ought to be laid on the horses," continued the driver. "Only when your attention is paid to the movements of the horses, will Your Majesty be able to speed up to a far distance."

"As you lagged behind, you had the intent to catch up with me; as you left me behind you, you were concerned that I would catch up and overtake you," added the driver. "In the driving race, you are either in front or behind. Under either circumstance, you all the time had your mind on me rather than on the horses. In that case, how could you focus on driving? That is why you dropped behind throughout the three sessions of the race."

——from *Han Fei Tzu*

Application

Calculation of gains or losses in the mind leads to absence of focus on what it should be laid on. Whatever you are up to, commitment or wholehearted devotion rather than the calculating of pros and cons contributes to your intended achievements.

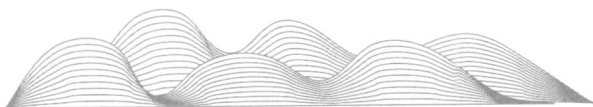

杨布击狗

　　杨朱之弟杨布素衣而出。天雨，解素衣，衣缁衣而反，其狗不知而吠之。杨布怒，将击之。杨朱曰："子毋击也，子亦犹是。曩者使女狗白而往，黑而来，子岂能毋怪哉？"

——《韩非子》

警言

　　当被误解的时候，应换位思考，站在他方角度去思考原因所在，这样更容易找到被误解的原因，从而消除误解。

Yang Bu to Hit at the Dog

Yang Bu, the younger brother of Yang Zhu, who was a famed Taoist from the state of Chu in the early period of Warring States, left home in white once. It rained later. Bu then took off his white clothes, dressed in black and came home. At the sight of the man clothed in black, the dog, not identifying him, then kept barking furiously at him. With intense rage, Bu was about to hit at the dog. At this very moment, Yang Zhu stopped him. "Don't hit at the dog since you are inclined to do the same thing," he reasoned. "If your dog left with white fur the other day and returned with black fur, wouldn't you feel strange about it?"

——from *Han Fei Tzu*

Application

As you were misunderstood, try to put yourself in the other party's shoe, finding out what was the matter with yourself. This may soon lead you to the reason why you were misperceived and then to removal of the misperception.

侏儒梦灶

卫灵公之时,弥子瑕有宠,专于卫国。侏儒有见公者曰:"臣之梦践矣。"公曰:"何梦?"对曰:"梦见灶,为见公也。"公怒曰:"吾闻见人主者梦见日,奚为见寡人而梦见灶?"对曰:"夫日兼烛天下,一物不能当也;人君兼烛一国人,一人不能拥也。故将见人主者梦见日。夫灶,一人炀焉,则后人无从见矣。今或者一人有炀君者乎?则臣虽梦见灶,不亦可乎!"

——《韩非子》

警 言

作为君王,偏听偏信误国;作为常人,偏听偏信误事或误人。多方面听取意见或建议,才能确保做出正确抉择。

Seeing the Cooking Stove in the Dream

King Ling of the state of Wei had a most preferred minister, Mi Zixia, who arrogated to himself all powers over the imperial court. A dwarf called on the king.

"One of my dreams has come true," reported the dwarf.

"What is the dream like?" the king enquired.

"I saw a cooking stove in my dream, which indicated I was going to meet Your Majesty," replied the small man.

"I hear that he who's going to meet the monarch tends to see the sun in his dream," raged the ruler of Wei.

"The sun, which will no way be shaded by any being in the world, illuminates every corner of the land," elucidated the dwarf. "Likewise, the monarch, the rays of whom will by no means be blocked by anyone, also shines upon every single subject in the state."

"Therefore, he who will pay a visit to the monarch sees the sun in his dream," he went on. "As for the cooking stove, if there is one man warming himself by the fire, no other men were able to sight the flare in the stove. At present, there is one man that hinders Your Majesty's rays from shining elsewhere, isn't there? In this case, can't I refer to Your Majesty as the cooking stove?"

——from *Han Fei Tzu*

Application

The monarch with an inclined ear is prone to put his kingdom in danger while an average person who has a biased ear is most likely to hold business up or have harm done to himself or others. Therefore, adoption of advice from all sides to a large extent leads to a well-reasoned decision.

不死之道

　　客有教燕王为不死之道者，王使人学之，所使学者未及学而客死。王大怒，诛之。王不知客之欺己，而诛学者之晚也。夫信不然之物而诛无罪之臣，不察之患也。且人所急无如其身，不能自使其无死，安能使王长生哉？

——《韩非子》

警　言

　　生老病死，天道所循，没有人能够走出五行之外而长生不老。追求长生之术，只是一种愿望，难以实现。认清这一天道，便能够辨认出"长生之术"的骗局。

The Practice of Immortality

A swindler, who claimed that he practised Tao in pursuit of immortality, came to the king of Yan with the information of immortality to be achieved through a certain practice. Informed of this, the king bade one of his subjects learn how to practise it. Nonetheless, before the one on the errand could do so the immortality pursuer breathed his last. This infuriated the king, who then had the man executed in a bid to quench his fury. The king of Yan failed to be aware that it was a fraud who tried to swindle him out of gold and silver, but issued an edict that the innocent subject be killed. Valuing much what, judging from common sense, was impossible, he had a life put to an end. What a fool he was! All men show the keener concern over themselves than any other one in the world. In this circumstance, as he was unable to sustain his own life through the practice of immortality, how could he be of any help to others who pursue immortal life?

——from *Han Fei Tzu*

Application

Birth, death, sickness and aging come in compliance with the law of nature, which no mortal beings are enabled to step beyond. Pursuit of immortality, as an elusive dream, subsists with the yearning for sustenance. Provided that the law of nature is identified, one can have a clarified perception of the fraud of immortality.

滥竽充数

　　齐宣王使人吹竽，必三百人。南郭处士请为王吹竽。宣王说之，廪食以数百人。宣王死，湣王立，好一一听之，处士逃。

——《韩非子》

警言

　　不学无术的人虽然能蒙混一时，但迟早会露出马脚。人只有通过勤学苦练而获得真才实学，才能经受住生活中的各种测试，安身立命。

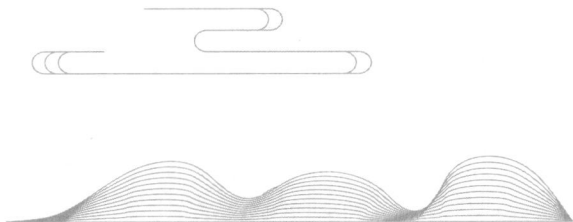

The Story of a Fake Reed-pipe Player

King Xuan of the state of Qi listened to a reed pipe ensemble of three hundred musicians altogether. Mr. Nanguo, a scholar, asked for a place in the orchestra, which was much to the king's delight, and was offered the pay worth a combined total of that of three hundred musicians. After King Xuan passed away, Prince Min came to the throne, known as King Min who loved solos to the contrary. Informed of this, the scholar took hurried flight.

——from *Han Fei Tzu*

Application

Whoever is incompetent may muddle through somehow for quite a time; however, his incapability will betray itself sooner or later. Only through painstaking effort, can one be well trained to be capable, endure all manner of ordeal, and establish himself in a certain career.

曾子杀猪

曾子之妻之市，其子随之而泣。其母曰："女还，顾反为女杀彘。"适市来，曾子欲捕彘杀之。妻止之曰："特与婴儿戏耳。"曾子曰："婴儿非与戏也。婴儿非有知也，待父母而学者也，听父母之教。今子欺之，是教子欺也。母欺子，子而不信其母，非以成教也。"

遂烹彘也。

——《韩非子》

警言

做人应言必有信，不能说一套而做一套，否则，长此以往将不得他人的信任。教育子女应言传身教，以诚教诚，否则难以令其信服不说，还会教出言不行、行不果的孩子。

Slaughtering the Pig to Fulfil the Promise

As Zeng Tzu's wife was about to go on her way to the market, their son clamoured to go with her.

"Stay home," wheedled the woman. "and I will slaughter the pig for dinner when I come home."

Upon her return, she found Zeng Tzu on the verge of stabbing at the pig, at which moment she held him back.

"I wasn't serious," she elaborated. ' I meant to quiet him down."

"You ought not to make an empty promise to a child," protested Zeng Tzu. "Children can't discern what is right or what is wrong, and they simply conduct themselves after the fashion of their parents as to what should be perceived as seemly or unseemly. The time you deceive the boy, you teach him to cheat. A mother cheats her son, which leads him to his distrust of Mother. This is by no means the right way of upbringing."

In order to fulfil his wife's promise to his son, Zeng Tzu thereby made a meal of the pig after all.

——from *Han Fei Tzu*

Application

Keep your word instead of breaking a promise made beforehand, or you will for certain lose trust of those who have ever received your promise. In terms of upbringing, you are supposed to exemplify your probity, moral beliefs and courtesy in your daily conducts. Ill examples corrupt even the best natural disposition, and it is in vain to give spoken instructions to your offspring, who tend to conduct themselves after the fashion of their parents, to behave by one rule, if you yourselves go by another.

画鬼最易

客有为齐王画者，齐王问曰："画孰最难者？"曰："犬马最难。""孰易者？"曰："鬼魅最易。"夫犬马，人所知也，旦暮罄于前，不可类之，故难。鬼魅，无形者，不罄于前，故易之也。

——《韩非子》

警 言

胡写乱画，是很简单的，胡编乱造用以欺骗那些没有见识的人，很容易；但若想恰如其分地展现出一个众人都熟知的事物，便不是那么容易的了。胡编乱造以欺骗见多识广的人，更不是那么容易的了。

Painting Ghosts with the Most Spared Effort

There lived an artist who was in the employ of the king of the state of Qi.

"To draw a picture," the king enquired, "what do you refer to as the hardest to paint?"

"The dog, the horse and the like," replied the artist.

"What is the easiest then?" the king continued asking.

"The ghost and the demon," was the answer.

As far as the dog and the horse are concerned, they are familiar to everyone, seen from morning to night. In this case, a likeness of a real dog or horse is prone to criticism, which is the justification for the difficulty in drawing the like subject. Ghosts and demons, in the eyes of the people, take no vivid form of any kind, invisible to all, which is less likely to incur disapproving comments. In this sense, the artist, painting things like them, runs little risk of being judged as regards his techniques or gift.

——from *Han Fei Tzu*

Application

To draw a hideous picture, an artist can spare much of his effort, which may be employed to fool the ill-informed. On the other hand, to give a full representation of what is widely known, an artist cannot spare an iota of his effort because a picture that is painted at random will by no means stir the heart of a well-informed person.

唇亡齿寒

晋献公以垂棘之璧假道于虞而伐虢，大夫宫之奇谏曰："不可。唇亡而齿寒，虞、虢相救，非相德也。今日晋灭虢，明日虞必随之亡。"虞君不听，受其璧而假之道。晋已取虢，还，反灭虞。

——《韩非子》

警 言

寓言中的虞王贪图小利，忽视了虢国与虞国相互依存的利害关系，而最终灭国。

The Lips and the Teeth

King Xian of the state of Jin meant to send troops through the state of Yu to encroach upon the state of Guo. In order for his troops to be let pass the land of Yu, he presented a precious piece of jade to the king of Yu, asking for the favour. As the king of Yu launched a discussion on whether it was right to let the Jin troops pass through their land, Gong Zhiqi, a senior official of Yu, objected to Jin's request.

"We can't give way to the Jin troops; for with lips gone, teeth go exposed to cold," Gong Zhiqi argued. "Yu and Guo that are to the rescue of each other are no way granting the other grace, but there is an inseparable bond between them in terms of political and military significance. Once Jin takes control of Guo, it will turn against us to wipe out the state of Yu soon afterward."

The king of Yu, who turned a deaf ear to this warning from Gong Zhiqi, accepted the gift of the precious jade from Jin and let its troops through. Presently, Jin seized the land of Guo, returned, and in turn captured the state of Yu.

——from *Han Fei Tzu*

Application

In this fable, the king of Yu, overwhelmed by minor gains, failed to take into consideration the fatal tie between the interested party of Guo and his own state, which led to the pathetic end of it.

讳疾忌医

扁鹊见蔡桓公,立有间。扁鹊曰:"君有疾在腠理,不治将恐深。"桓侯曰:"寡人无。"扁鹊出。桓侯曰:"医之好治不病以为功。"居十日,扁鹊复见曰:"君之病在肌肤,不治将益深。"桓侯不应。扁鹊出。桓侯又不悦。居十日,扁鹊复见曰:"君之病在肠胃,不治将益深。"桓侯又不应。扁鹊出。桓侯又不悦。居十日,扁鹊望桓侯而还走,桓侯故使人问之。扁鹊曰:"病在腠理,汤熨之所及也;在肌肤,针石之所及也;在肠胃,火齐之所及也;在骨髓,司命之所属,无奈何也。今在骨髓,臣是以无请也。"居五日,桓侯体痛,使人索扁鹊,已逃秦矣。桓侯遂死。故良医之治病也,攻之于腠理。此皆争之于小者也。夫事之祸福亦有腠理之地,故圣人蚤从事焉。

——《韩非子》

警 言

不要回避问题,因为掩饰自身的缺点,会导致问题变得一发而不可收。听取专业人士的建议,接受问题的存在,在问题变大之前使势态得以控制,这才是面对问题时应持有的正确态度。

The Taboo Subject of Disease
and Seeing the Doctor

Bianque called to pay his respects to King Huan of the state of Qi. Standing a while, Bianque reported to the duke, "Your Majesty, you have trouble brewing in the surface, which will worsen if not treated."

"Nonsense," protested the king.

"Doctors are disposed to treat the non-diseased for achievements to their credit," he remarked after Bianque left.

Ten days later, Bianque came to pay his respects once again.

"Your Majesty, your disease remains in the skin, and will go deeper into your internal organs if not treated," reported the doctor a second time, to whom the king, overwhelmed with rage, did not respond at all. Bianque left.

As another ten days passed, Bianque paid his visit a third time.

"Your Majesty, your illness has reached intestines and stomach, and will deteriorate if not treated," reported the famed doctor.

Upon the doctor's words, King Huan, getting terribly annoyed, gave no response. Then left the doctor.

With the passage of another ten days, Bianque saw from far the king and took to his heels. The king wondered why the doctor evaded the meeting with him, sending a man to enquire as regards the reason.

"When in the surface, the disease can be treated with a wash or steam by a decoction of medicinal ingredients; while in the skin, it can be done away with by way of acupuncture; as it is in intestines and stomach, there is a cure for it by taking a decoction to clear away heat and fire inside the body; once in the bones, the disease stretches beyond the capability of a doctor, but to the domain of God of Fate. Now that the king has been diseased into the bones, I won't ask to treat him."

Five days after that, King Huan felt a sudden pang in his body, sending for Bianque, who had run away to the state of Qin. The king's life came to an end because of his disease.

A good doctor, who chooses to conduct his treatment when the disease brews in the surface, is endeavouring to settle a problem while it remains in the embryonic stage. Weal and woe that an event may bring to being may take shape in the initial phase, of which sages opt to dispose as soon as possible.

——from *Han Fei Tzu*

Application

An evasion of issues with concealment of one's defects may lead to the aggravation of them. Listen to professionals' advice, accept the existence of issues and then you will be likely to bring matters under control before they go worse. This is the right attitude to any issue that waits to be solved.

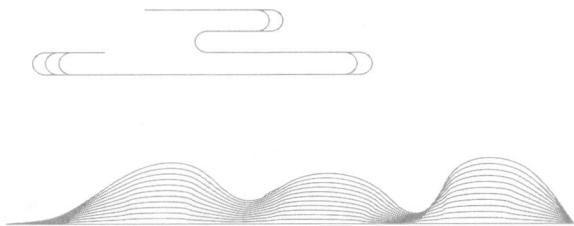

不死之药

　　有献不死之药于荆王者,谒者操之以入。中射之士问曰:"可食乎?"曰:"可。"因夺而食之。王大怒,使人杀中射之士,中射之士使人说王曰:"臣问谒者,曰'可食',臣故食之,是臣无罪而罪在谒者也,且客献不死之药,臣食之而王杀臣,是死药也,是客欺王也。夫杀无罪之臣而明人之欺王也,不如释臣。"王乃不杀。

——《韩非子》

警 言

　　谏言所采取的方式非常重要,以幽默、智慧的方式进行既能够让谏言得以接受,又能够令进谏者全身而退。

The Story of the Elixir

An elixir was presented to the king of Chu, delivered by the herald to the royal palace. "Edible?" questioned a palace guard.

"Yes," replied the herald.

The guard then seized and swallowed the elixir. Upon this, the king, blazed with fury, sent his men to slay the guard for his malpractice. This guard in turn had someone reason with the king on his behalf.

"I enquired the herald whether it was good to eat, who said it was, and I thereby swallowed it. This showcases that it was not I but the herald who was supposed to accept the perpetration. Furthermore, the elixir that was conveyed to the king was said to enable man to have an eternal life. Now as I have had it and am faced with execution on the king's order, this suggests the so-called elixir was not for life but for death. That shows the elixir-presenter was taking in Your Majesty. You want a guiltless life to prove you are deceived by the presenter. You may as well let me go." The king thereby pronounced the guard's life unwanted.

——from *Han Fei Tzu*

Application

The fashion in which we give advice is of paramount importance, which, if of humour and wisdom, most inclines one to acceptance, bringing to the suggestion maker an unharmed end.

狗猛酒酸

　　宋人有酤酒者，升概甚平，遇客甚谨，为酒甚美，县帜甚高著，然不售，酒酸。怪其故，问其所知。问长者杨倩，倩曰："汝狗猛耶？"曰："狗猛则酒何故而不售？"曰："人畏焉。或令孺子怀钱挈壶瓮而往酤，而狗迓而龁之，此酒所以酸而不售也。"

—— 《韩非子》

警言

　　环境影响事物的发展。在恶劣的环境下，即使事物本身质量再好，有时也难以得到应有的认可和发展。在社会生活的各个方面，环境均影响着人的发展。

The Fierce Dog and the Sour Wine

There was a brewer in the state of Song, who made nice wine, employed a handsome measuring cup for wine selling, received customers warmly, and had the sign hung up high, making it eye-catching. Nonetheless, his wine, said to be sour, sold poorly, at which the brewer wondered so much. Pining for the reason, the man went to an elder, Yang Qian, with whom he had had some acquaintance.

"Do you have a ferocious dog?" enquired the elderly man.

"Yes," responded the brewer.

"Yet what does it have to do with wine selling?" wondered the brewer.

"People are afraid of your dog," explained Yang Qian. "When a boy is sent to buy your wine, the dog goes at him, inclined to bite. That is why your wine doesn't sell and goes sour."

——from *Han Fei Tzu*

Application

The environment decides how and in what direction things develop. Negative ambience can hardly provide a thing or person with chance of being recognized or developed. No matter what aspect of social life it is associated with, the social environment has a critical effect on the development of a person.

自相矛盾

楚人有鬻盾与矛者，誉之曰："吾盾之坚，物莫能陷也。"又誉其矛曰："吾矛之利，于物无不陷也。"或曰："以子之矛陷子之盾，何如？"其人弗能应也。夫不可陷之盾与无不陷之矛，不可同世而立。

——《韩非子》

警 言

世上不可能同时存在不可破的盾和无坚不摧的矛，任何事物都有自身的缺陷，忽略了缺陷而过分夸大优点，则是对客观事物规律的不尊重。

The Best Spear and the Best Shield

There lived a man in the state of Chu, who sold shields and spears for a living.

"My shields are sturdy," the man said boastingly, "and you can find nothing to pierce through them."

"My spears are so sharp that they will be able to pierce through whatever it is," he went on with his boast.

"If you poke your spear into your shield, what will happen then?" queried a passer-by.

The seller could not afford him an answer. There is little chance of the coexistence of a shield that endures all manner of spears and a spear that can overcome all shields.

——from *Han Fei Tzu*

Application

The sturdiest shield cannot run concurrently with the spear that can pierce through any shield, either having a certain defect. When overstating the power of something or somebody in ignorance of the weakness, you are believed to lack logic or senses.

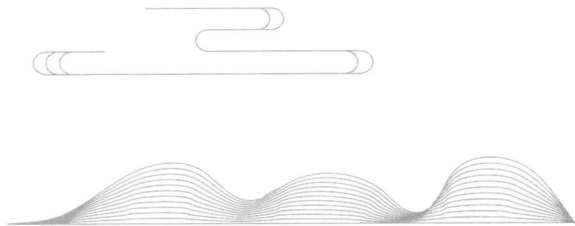

买椟还珠

楚人有卖其珠于郑者，为木兰之椟，薰以桂椒，缀以珠玉，饰以玫瑰，辑以翡翠。郑人买其椟而还其珠。此可谓善卖椟矣，未可谓善鬻珠也。

——《韩非子》

警言

人往往被纷繁花哨的事物表象所迷惑，分不清主次，厘不出重点，从而最终没有得到对于人生来说最重要的东西。透过现象而深入本质，这本身就是人要学习的。能够透过现象而透视到本质的人，必将活得精彩。

Buying the Casket Without the Pearls

A man who was from the state of Chu sold pearls in the state of Zheng. He made a casket out of magnolia wood, scented with such spices as osmanthus and pepper, inlaid with jewels and jade, ornamented with roses, and edged with kingfisher's plumes.

A local man purchased the casket, leaving behind the pearls. This seller, who may be credited with the capability to equip his casket with grace, deserves no credit for selling pearls.

——from *Han Fei Tzu*

Application

Easily bewildered by the gaudy looks, people tend not to identify what are major events to take priority over minor affairs, as a consequence of which, they will not be able to be equipped with the grand elements of life. To see through the appearance to perceive the essence is a significant practice in life. As for all those who can take a grasp of the primary ingredients of life, their chance of living a fruitful life is far greater.

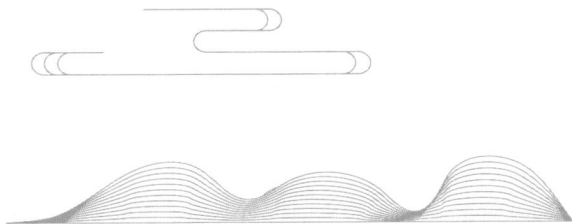

守株待兔

宋人有耕田者。田中有株,兔走触株,折颈而死,因释其耒而守株,冀复得兔。兔不可复得,而身为宋国笑。

——《韩非子》

警言

不付出努力而获得,只是一种侥幸。任何意外的收获,都不能作为可以遵守的规则照抄使用。不知道变通地去推行狭隘的经验,结果只能是一无所获。

Waiting for a Hare to Crash into a Stump

In the state of Song there lived a husbandman who tilled land for a living. In the field where he toiled remained a tree stump, against which a hare dashed forward with its neck fractured, dead. Leaving behind his hoe, the tiller thereafter stayed by the stump in the hope that one more hare would come up. The occurrence that he came across a neck-broken hare did not repeat itself, and a deliberate copy of this made a laughing-stock of himself across the state.

——from *Han Fei Tzu*

Application

It is by luck that anything is obtained without effort. Any achievement reached with little effort ought not to be referred to as a case of success, in which the achievement is only made by chance. In compliance with a law concluded based on one accidental experience, you are getting nowhere in the final analysis.

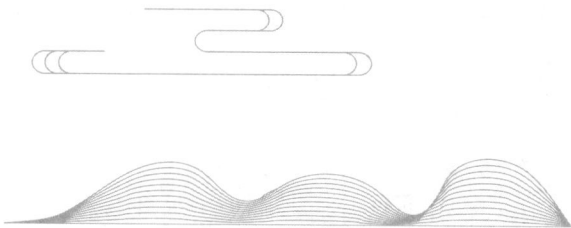

郑人买履

郑人有且置履者,先自度其足而置之其坐,至之市而忘操之。已得履;乃曰:"吾忘持度。"反归取之。及反,市罢,遂不得履。人曰:"何不试之以足?"曰:"宁信度,无自信也。"

——《韩非子》

警言

基于实际出发的判断,就是准确的。买履的郑人恰恰抛弃了随身携带的客观标准,而去寻找已经量好的标准,是死守教条的表现。无论有没有现成的规矩,只要从实际出发,随机应变,一样可以解决问题。因此,我们说话、做事,不要只从书本出发,不要仅仅遵循成规,而是要灵活变通,以事实为基准,这样的行事才是科学的。

Buying Shoes with Reference to the Measure

A man who came from the state of Zheng was going to buy shoes. He measured his feet, leaving the measure on his seat, before he went out to the market. Upon arriving there, it came to his mind that he left the measure behind.

"Why, I don't have the measure with me," he regretted, with the shoes he picked in hand.

He hurried on his way home for the measure. By the time he returned to the market, the fair was over, which led to his failure to buy shoes.

"Why did you not try the shoes on?" queried another man.

"I'd rather be assured of the measure than of my feet," replied the purchaser.

——from *Han Fei Tzu*

Application

A judgment made based on facts endures all manner of tests. The purchaser in the fable abandons for reference what is with him wherever he goes as the ruler, but refers to the measure, which betrays his inflexibility. Whether there is a rule or not to abide by, you will be able to dispose of issues as long as you take into consideration the actual facts. Therefore, books or set rules should not be identified as the reference by which we conduct ourselves. Instead, reference to the facts is the only criterion on the basis of which we act.

弓与箭

一人曰:"吾弓良,无所用矢!"一人曰:"吾矢善,无所用弓!"羿闻之曰:"非弓何以往矢?非矢何以中的?"会合弓矢,而教之射。

——《韩非子》

警言

这则寓言故事强调了合作与相互依赖的重要性。无论是在生活中还是专业领域中,都应注重与他人的合作和协调,借用对方的优势,形成更大的力量,以实现既定的或更大的目标。

The Bow and the Arrow

"So good is my bow that requires no arrow!" a man claimed.

"So good is my arrow that requires no bow!" asserted another man.

Hou Yi, a most skilled archer, heard them and questioned, "Without a bow, with what do you shoot your arrow? Without an arrow, with what do you hit the target?"

Putting both the bow and the arrow together, Hou Yi taught the two men how to shoot through the combined use of both.

——from *Han Fei Tzu*

Application

As this fable intimates, emphasis ought to be laid on the significance of cooperation and interdependence. Whether in everyday life or in some professional areas, cooperation and coordination, which are aimed at employing the other's advantage or strength to compensate for what you are lacking in, can lead you and the other party to the achievement of the set or bigger aim.

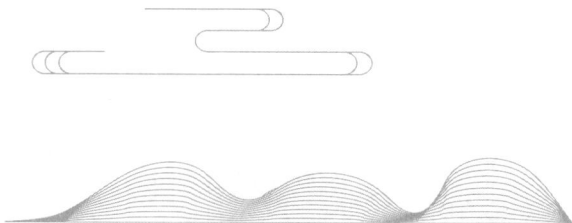

水蛇装神

泽涸，蛇将徙。有小蛇谓大蛇曰："子行而我随之，人以为蛇之行者，必有杀子。不如相衔负我以行，人以我为神君也。"乃相衔负以越公道。人皆避之，曰："神君也。"

——《韩非子》

警言

不论是自然世界，还是在社会生活中，均不要被表面现象所麻痹，而要深入理解事物的本质，才能避免被欺骗或误导。

Two Water Snakes in the Disguise of a God

As a marsh was drying up, two snakes planned to move house.

"If you are in the lead with me to follow," said a small snake to a large one, "man will be aware that it is snakes that are moving and someone will kill you. You'd better carry me on your back, each of us holding the other's tail in the mouth." They thereby did as they discussed. Seeing this, people got away from them and said, "That's a god."

——from *Han Fei Tzu*

Application

In not only the nature but also the human world, it is easy to be tricked by one's disguise or masquerade. Resort to wisdom, an investigation into what's behind the scene, and an improved understanding of what comes in sight may save us from being misled or fraud in either interactions between people or academic studies.

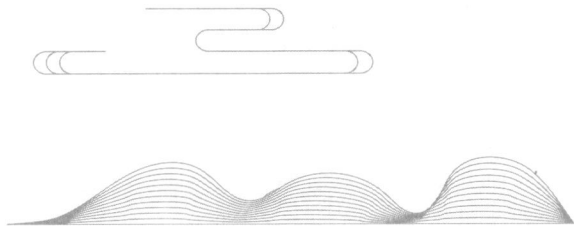

御者之变

　　晏子为齐相,出,其御之妻从门间而窥,其夫为相御,拥大盖,策驷马,意气扬扬,甚自得也。既而归,其妻请去。夫问其故,妻曰:"晏子长不满六尺,身相齐国,名显诸侯。今者妾观其出,志念深矣,常有以自下者。今子长八尺,乃为人仆御;然子之意,自以为足。妾是以求去也。"

　　其后,夫自抑损。晏子怪而问之,御以实对。晏子荐以为大夫。

——《晏子春秋》

警 言

　　志向高远的人,往往谦虚谨慎,谦逊低调;胸无大志的人则往往容易满足现状,盲目自大。

The Coachman's Change

One day, Yan Tzu, prime minister of the state of Qi, went out in his carriage. His coachman's wife, peeking through the gate, saw her husband: he was complacent and conceited under the grand awning of the carriage pulled by four horses.

Upon his return, the coachman's wife asked to divorce him, and his husband enquired why.

"Prime minister of Qi as Yan Tzu is and famed as he is among the nobility," his wife explained, "he, a man of great ambition, does not behave himself with airs and graces. You are just a coachman, and yet you conduct yourself, conceited and contented. That's why I seek to leave you."

After this, her husband assumed a look of modesty, which was to Yan Tzu's surprise. When Yan Tzu then enquired as to what was behind the alteration, the coachman told him the truth, who was later recommended by Yan Tzu for an official post.

——from *Spring and Autumn by Yan Tzu*

Application

Men of great ambition tend to be modest with a low profile while those of little determination to achieve much incline to satisfaction from achievement of diminutive worth, thereby conceited.

黄金万两

　　齐人有东郭敞者，犹多愿，愿有万金。其徒请假焉，不与，曰："吾将以求封也。"其徒怒而去之宋。曰："此爱于无也，故不如以先与之有也。"

——《商君书》

警言

　　这则寓言告诉我们，不要空想，要脚踏实地。与其将希望寄托在缥缈的未来，则不如把握当下，做好手边的事，做好今天的事，让你的钱财真正地发挥作用，或者把握眼前的机遇，实现容易达成的目标。

Ten Thousand Taels of Gold

There lived a man named Dongguo Chang in the state of Qi, who mentioned about his wide range of aspirations, one of which was that he desired to hold in possession ten thousand taels of gold. A student of his made a request for the favour of a small loan, but with a refusal in answer. "I'm going to exchange the money for a government post," specified Dongguo. Overwhelmed with rage for these words, his student decided to leave him for the state of Song and paid him a visit before his departure. "You spare what remains to be had," he said. "You may let the money play a more practical role if you lend it to me."

——from *Shang Tzu*

Application

This fable conveys to us the moral that a dream may come in vain but an action leads to an achievement. We had better seize the present moment than lay your hope on the far future with a prospect of any certain accomplishment. Complete your mission at hand, cast your fortune in an active role and grasp the opportunity present in a bid to achieve the goals that you perceive as achievable.

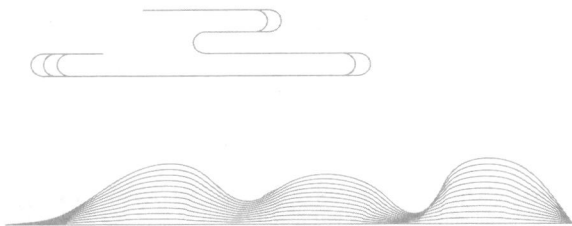

皮之不存，毛将焉附

魏文侯出游，见路人反裘而负刍。文侯曰："胡为反裘而负刍？"对曰："臣爱其毛。"

文侯曰："若不知其里尽而毛无所恃耶？"

——《新序》

警言

若事物得以存在的基础动摇了，事物也无法继续存在。这告诉我们，倘若国家遭到侵略，领土尽失，那么国人的利益乃至生命也将无法得到保障。

The Fur and the Hide

King Wen of the state of Wei on a tour of the country came across a man who was wearing a fur-lined jacket with the hide out and carrying a bundle of straw.

"Why have the fur inside while carrying straw?" enquired the king.

"I have a preference for the fur," replied the man.

"Well, don't you realize," elaborated King Wen, "that as the hide wears out, the fur can find nowhere to stay."

——from *New Discourse*

Application

Given that the base on which a thing survives is damaged, the thing itself won't last any longer. This fable conveys to us the inspiration that if our country were taken by another, our good and even our lives would not endure with the loss of the foundation where we and our possessions come from.

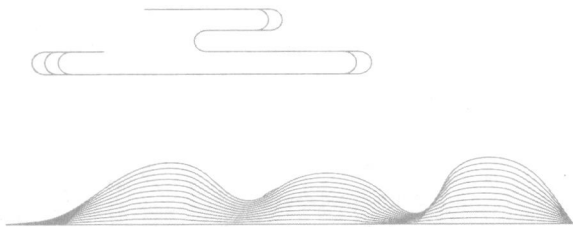

中国寓言故事选英译

叶公好龙

　　叶公子高好龙，钩以写龙，凿以写龙，居室雕文以写龙。于是夫天龙闻而下之，窥头于牖，拖尾于堂。叶公见之，弃而还走，失其魂魄，无色无主。是叶公非好龙也，好夫似龙而非龙者也。

——《新序》

警 言

　　这个故事告诉我们，了解一样事物须深入，而非流于表面，否则当面临考察时，会将真相暴露。

Lord Ye's Profession of Love for Dragons

Lord Ye, whose given name was Zigao, was enthusiastic about dragons, which were painted on his girdles, were carved on his wine cups and patterned all his residence. Informed of this, the dragon himself came down to Lord Ye from heaven, head through the door and tail through the window. Upon seeing this, the lord fled, frightened out of his senses. As was the case, Lord Ye had no liking for the genuine dragon but for the artificial.

——from *New Discourse*

Application

This fable conveys to us the idea that a deepened knowledge of something is vital for one to have. With a superficial perception of it, one's disguised love is more likely to be embarrassedly exposed in face of a test.

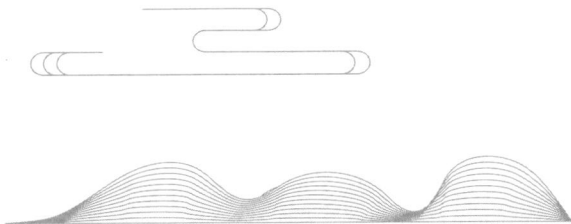

曲突徙薪

客有过主人者，见其灶直突，旁有积薪，客谓主人，更为曲突，远徙其薪，不者且有火患。主人嘿然不应。俄而家果失火。邻里共救之，幸而得息。于是杀牛置酒，谢其邻人，灼烂者在于上行，馀客以功次坐，而不录言曲突者。人谓主人曰："乡使听客之言，不费牛酒，终亡火患。今论功而请客，曲突徙薪亡恩泽，焦头烂额为上客耶？"主人乃寤而请之。

——《汉书》

警 言

这则故事告诉我们不应执拗于自己的偏见，要有开放的胸怀，谦虚地听取他人的意见，这样能够防止个人偏见可能带来的恶果。同时，我们也要感恩，一颗感恩的心能够带来更大、更多的善果。

Good Advice Ignored

A man walking past a house noticed that the chimney was going straight upward from the stove, with a pile of firewood stacked by. The man said to the owner of the house, "You had better build a bend in the chimney and move the fuel away. Otherwise, your house may catch fire." The owner of the house gave no response. Shortly afterward, the house was on fire. All neighbours came to help put out the fire, which, fortunately, was quenched. In a bid to extend gratitude to the neighbours, the house owner killed an ox and set a feast. At the feast, the ones whose burns were the severest were arranged in the honour seats, the remainder of the guests seated in sequence of priorities with no mention made of the man who advised them to add a bend to the chimney.

"Provided that you had taken that man's advice," someone said to the house owner, "you could have averted the disaster, let alone the expenditure on the ox and wine. When you are entertaining those who gave a helping hand, honouring those with worst burns, how can you miss out on the entertaining list the one who warned you of fire?"

This brought the owner of house to an awareness of his negligence, who then invited the adviser.

——from *The History of Han Dynasty*

Application

This story warns us not to stubbornly adhere to our opinion, but to have a modest mind open to good advice, which, once taken, may save one from adversity or severe fruit. Besides, it is advisable that one be grateful to those who ever offered constructive suggestions or gave a helping hand. Gratitude shown to them is not only a display of a kind heart but also an approach to attending to interpersonal affairs, bringing bigger, more good fruit.

伯牙碎琴

伯牙鼓琴,钟子期听之。方鼓琴而志在太山,钟子期曰:"善哉乎鼓琴! 巍巍乎若太山。"少选之间,而志在流水,钟子期又曰:"善哉乎鼓琴! 汤汤乎若流水。"钟子期死,伯牙破琴绝弦,终身不复鼓琴,以为世无足复为鼓琴者。

——《吕氏春秋》

警 言

知音难觅。不仅弹琴是这样,用人也是这样。即便是对有贤德的人,如果不以礼相待,有贤德的人又怎会尽忠呢?

Bo Ya Breaking Guqin

While Bo Ya was playing the Guqin, a seven-stringed plucked instrument similar to a zither, Zhong Ziqi was listening. As the tune was transporting the audience to the scramble up a great mountain, Ziqi offered a critical acclaim.

"What a virtuoso!" exclaimed this captivated listener. "It sounds like I am being brought onto the adventure of climbing a high mountain."

After a while, the strings were plucked in representation of the billows speeding forward, which Ziqi thought highly of.

"What craft!" appraised the enchanted one. "The tune flows as if I were conveyed to the surging rapids."

No sooner had Zhong Ziqi passed away than Bo Ya crushed into shreds his stringed musical instrument, its strings broken. He, who held that the world would find no one worth the tune he played, never touched the Guqin for the rest of his life.

——from *Spring and Autumn by Lv Buwei*

Application

As the fable goes, it rarely takes place that someone who has a deepened understanding and is appreciative of one's tune is found. Not only does it apply to music appreciation, but it is true of seeking talents. Men of virtue as they are, if not treated with due respect, how can it be likely that men of talent pay their loyalty, committed to their duties?

荆人夜涉

荆人欲袭宋，使人先表澭水。澭水暴益，荆人弗知，循表而夜涉，溺死者千有余人，军惊而坏都舍。向其先表之时可导也，今水已变而益多矣，荆人尚犹循表而导之，此其所以败也。今世之主法先王之法也，有似于此。其时已与先王之法亏矣，而曰此先生之法也，而法之，以此为治，岂不悲哉？

——《吕氏春秋》

警 言

事物都是不断发展的，不能静止地看问题。随着时间的推移，时移世易，解决问题的方法也要随之变化，否则会酿成大错。

Wading the River by Night

The state of Chu schemed to launch a surprise attack upon the state of Song, to do which the Chu troops had to cross the Yong River. Therefore, men were assigned to measure the depth of the river. Known as the depth was, the Yong River saw a sudden rise to a fiercely high level. Having little idea of it, the Chu troops, following the mark made before the increase in water level, waded the river in the night, more than a thousand soldiers drowned in water. Startled and frightened, the troops collapsed in the same way that houses came down. When the mark was set at the outset, it was practicable for the men to pass the river. However, with the rise of the water, the troops of Chu tried to cross the river in compliance with the previously made sign, which led to their failure in going across the river. Like the Chu troops wading the river by night, the monarch of the present time conforms to the law that the late king was practising. As regards what comes as an issue in the present reign, the old law, which the current king keeps to and which he derives from the late king, has been found to an awkward use. Isn't it pathetic to rule a state with the old law sticked to?

——from *Spring and Autumn by Lv Buwei*

Application

All things in the world are set in motion as the river rises and falls, which brings a dynamic view of the world to being. With the passage of time, the earth, the world, and the people go on vicissitudes. The right way to settle an issue that comes up is to see it from a changing, changeable and changed perspective, or a sad ending will be brought about.

刻舟求剑

　　楚人有涉江者,其剑自舟中坠于水,遽契其舟,曰:"是吾剑之所从坠。"舟止,从其所契者入水求之。舟已行矣,而剑不行,求剑若此,不亦惑乎?

——《吕氏春秋》

警 言

　　世间万物,总是处于不断变化的过程中,若以静止的眼光来看待变化发展的事物,必将导致错误的判断。因此,无论是教育、处理人际关系抑或治国,教条、拘泥成法、固执、不懂得变通必将导致失败。

Marking the Boat to Locate the Sword

A man, who was from the state of Chu, was ferrying across the river when his sword dropped into the water. Without delay, he made a mark where the sword fell over into the waves. "This is where my sword dropped," he assured himself. The moment the boat berthed, he hastened into the water for his sword from the marked place. The boat had moved while the lost sword remained in the part of the river where it fell. In this circumstance, no matter how hard he struggled for the sword, his effort was bound to go fruitless. Wasn't he of confused wits?

——from *Spring and Autumn by Lv Buwei*

Application

Viewed with an invariable eye, a misjudgment may be drawn about everything in the world on the constant change. Therefore, with regards to from education to interpersonal relations to ruling a country, dogmatism and inflexibility will, in the most probability, lead to failure.

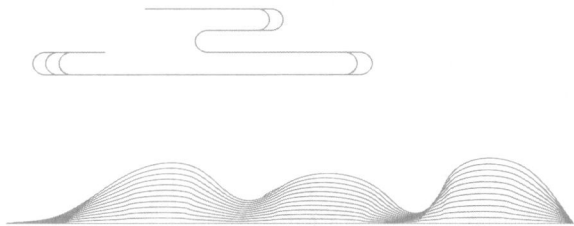

宋人御马

宋人有取道者，其马不进，倒而投之鸂水。又复取道，其马不进，又到而投之鸂水。如此者三。虽造父之所以威马，不过此矣。不得造父之道，而徒得其威，无益于御。

——《吕氏春秋》

警 言

不贤德的人做君主，只耍威而不施德。威严越多，人民越不服从，反抗日益。因此，虽然威严不可无，也不可仅仅依赖威严。做君主如此，做人也如此。不能失去威严而任人摆布，也不可过于威严而让人无法靠近。

Driving a Horse

A traveller, who came from the state of Song, hurried on his way while his horse refused to advance. He then urged it down into a stream, threatening to kill it. Back on the road he attempted to force it forward on its back, but the horse was still unwilling to make any advance. Again the man urged it into the water. This happened three times in total. Even Zao Fu, a skillful horse driver, could resort to no better means than to overpower a horse into obedience. However, the man from the state of Song learnt to bully or threaten instead of learning how Zao Fu drove or rode a horse, which wouldn't do good to horse control.

——from *Spring and Autumn by Lv Buwei*

Application

Admittedly, a man of no virtue exerted his authority without mercy or humanity. With more rigidity but less grace, the subjects would not submit to his rule, which may escalate into increased uprise. Therefore, while authority is required, a ruler cannot resort to nothing but authority, which is true of an average social being. You cannot lose dignity, held at the mercy of others, but meanwhile you should not make yourself unapproachable due to your overdue self-respect.

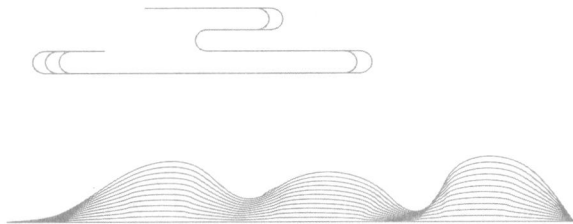

宣王好射

齐宣王好射,说人之谓己能用强弓也。其尝所用不过三石,以示左右,左右皆试引之,中关而止。皆曰:"此不下九石,非王其孰能用是?"宣王之情,所用不过三石,而终身自以为用九石,岂不悲哉!

——《吕氏春秋》

警 言

如果总是满足于别人的赞美,而不愿意面对自己的缺点,那么人就无法真正进步。因此,若想在某个领域取得成就,就须正视自己的不足,并努力改进。

The King and His Bow

King Xuan of the state of Qi was a keen archer who loved to be commended as a powerful bowman. As a matter of fact, he could draw a bow no heavier than thirty catties. The time he showed a bow to his attendants, they pulled it for a try, but halfway to the full extent. "It must weigh no less than ninety catties," the attendants exclaimed. "None but Your Majesty has the power to use so heavy a bow." The actual weight of King Xuan's bow is thirty catties, the professed weight ninety catties. That's pathetic.

——from *Spring and Autumn by Lv Buwei*

Application

King Xuan took delight in the name to gain, sacrificing his chance to perfect his shooting skill. Given that one finds satisfaction in compliments and praises, disposed not to face up to his own demerits, he will hardly have occasion to make advances. To achieve something in a certain field, you will have to look into yourself, face your weaknesses, and go all out to overcome them.

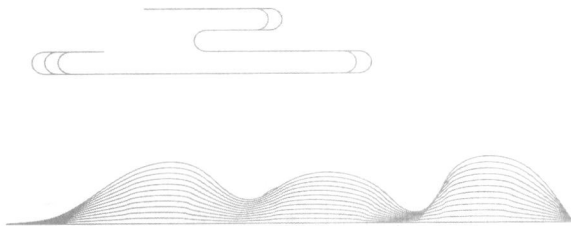

掩耳盗钟

范氏之亡也，百姓有得钟者。欲负而走，则钟大不可负。以椎毁之，钟况然有音。恐人闻之而夺己也，遽掩其耳。恶人闻之可也，恶己自闻之，悖矣。

——《吕氏春秋》

凡是客观存在，不会依人的主观意志而改变。倘若对客观现实不正视，而是闭目塞听，结果是自欺欺人、遭人嘲笑。

Stopping Up Ears to Steal the Bell

The house of Fan, an aristocratic family, fled, whose bell chanced to be in the hold of a man. The man had the intent to take it away on his back, the bell too large to bear. A hammer used to break it, the bell clanged. Afraid to be heard and caught red-handed, he stopped up his ears in haste. His fear to be heard by others is reasonable while it does not make any sense that he fears he himself could hear the clang.

—— from *Spring and Autumn by Lv Buwei*

Application

Any objective being, independent of the human will, sustains itself. Your disregard shown for what exists as the objective being, eyes shut and deaf ears turned to it, leads to self-deceit and ridicule.

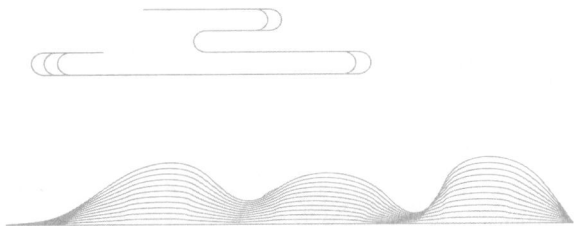

投婴于江

有过于江上者,见人方引婴儿而欲投之江中,婴儿啼。人问其故。曰:"此其父善游。"其父虽善游,其子岂遽善游哉?以此任物,亦必悖矣。

——《吕氏春秋》

警言

技能的掌握并非遗传而得,而是通过自身的学习而获得的。因此,个人如果希望成长,培养能力,则需要后天不断地学习。

An Infant Let Swim

A man walking along the river bank saw someone on the verge of flinging into the water an infant, who then cried a loud cry with terror. "Why are you throwing the child into the river?" some passers-by enquired of the man. "His father is a good swimmer," he rejoined. A father is a good swimmer, and does it follow that his son was born a good swimmer? It is absurd that one attends to business in this fashion.

—— from *Spring and Autumn by Lv Buwei*

Application

One is equipped with skills in some fields, not through genetic codes but as a result of acquired learning. As a consequence, any individual, who aspires to encourage his personal growth or develop his capacity, is supposed to go on fresh adventures aimed at new skills or knowledge.

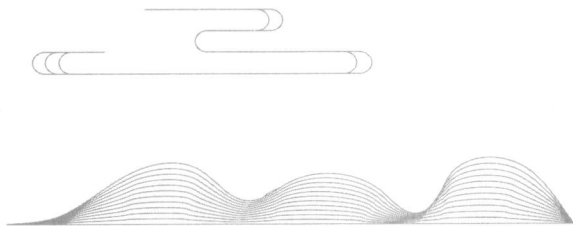

次非杀蛟

荆有次非者,得宝剑于干遂。还反涉江,至于中流,有两蛟夹绕其船,次非谓舟人曰:"子尝见两蛟绕船能两活者乎?"船人曰:"未之见也。"次非攘臂祛衣,拔宝剑曰:"此江中之腐肉朽骨也!弃剑以全己,余奚爱焉!"于是赴江刺蛟,杀之而复上船。舟中之人皆得活。荆王闻之,仕之执圭。

——《吕氏春秋》

警 言

迎难而上、藐视困难的人,往往绝处逢生。反之,畏惧困难,节节后退,坐以待毙,则会没有生机。为人处世也好,国家之间的较量也罢,均可习之矣。

Killing Flood Dragons

There lived a man named Ci Fei from the state of Chu, who once chanced to hold in possession a sword at Gansui of the state of Wu (Northwest of Soochou, Jiangsu Province today). As he was crossing the river midstream on his way back to his hometown, two flood dragons pressed from two sides toward the boat he was in, and twirled around it. At the sight of all this, Ci Fei questioned the boatman, "With the boat entangled by the two dragons, will the two big things and men onboard both survive?"

"No, neither will do," responded the boatman.

Rolling up his sleeves, Fei stretched out his arms to tuck up the front part of his robe. With a clank, he drew out his sword.

"The worst is that I may end in rotten flesh and decayed bones in the river. If the loss of a sword leads to self-protection, why am I loath to give up just a weapon?" Fei raged.

The man of valour thereby plunged himself into the billows to stab at the dragons, after which he regained the boat with all the lives on board safe and sound.

In praise of the anecdote of Ci Fei's, the king of Chu bestowed upon him a title of nobility.

—— from *Spring and Autumn by Lv Buwei*

Application

Those who brave and rise to difficulties are liable to have access to rescue or escape from death. On the contrary, it is unlikely that you gain access to blessings or rescue at the critical moment if you do not fight for your chance in adversity. This applies to either how you conduct yourself in the earthly world or how to dispose of international relations.

凿井得人

宋之丁氏，家无井而出溉汲，常一人居外。及其家穿井，告人曰："吾穿井得一人。"有闻而传之者曰："丁氏穿井得一人。"国人道之，闻之于宋君。宋君令人问之于丁氏。丁氏对曰："得一人之使，非得一人于井中也。"求能之若此，不若无闻也。

——《吕氏春秋》

警言

不应轻信传言，而应该通过理性分析或亲自考察来辨别信息的真伪。更不要盲目传播，以免以讹传讹。

Digging a Well and Getting a Man

There was a man surnamed Ding in the state of Song, and water had to be fetched from somewhere else because of there being no well in his yard. In this circumstance, one of his family members was compelled to keep outside for water every single day. Later some time, they had a well of their own, which saved one man from fetching water all the time. Now the man mentioned to whoever he met, "I've got a man for labor since I dug a well." This spread quickly. As the statement spread, it went further from what it was like. As it went, "The Dings dug out a living man." It became the subject of people's conversation and finally reached the ruler of Song, who sent for the man, seeking to know what had really happened. "I said that I got a man for labor, but not that I dug out a man from under the ground," explained the man. As is understood, it is better to be ill-informed than to be told of hearsay.

—— from *Spring and Autumn by Lv Buwei*

Application

Hearsay or the rumour should be given enough consideration and investigation to find out whether it is credible or incredible. Moreover, it is stupid to spread it without a sure knowledge of the likelihood whether or not it may be hurtful or even destructive.

生木造屋

　　高阳应将为室家,匠对曰:"未可也。木尚生,加涂其上,必将挠。以生为室,今虽善,后将必败。"高阳应曰:"缘子之言,则室不败也。木枯则益劲,涂干则益轻,以益劲任益轻,则不败。"匠人无辞而对,受令而为之。室之始成也善,其后果败。高阳应好小察,而不通乎大理也。

——《吕氏春秋》

警 言

　　在工作和生活中,听取他人意见非常重要,他人的意见或建议往往能够让我们规避一些常识性或者专业性的错误。此外,对于客观规律以及常识,我们应该予以尊重。

A Mansion Made of Raw Wood

Gao Yangying couldn't wait to have his mansion built with the trees freshly cut down. The lumber ready though, the construction worker refused to start building.

"It won't do. If the house is built with the newly cut wood, it will go bent some day in the future with mud applied to the outside of the wood. Built with raw wood, the house may be looking steady at present, but it will crumble sooner or later," specified the worker.

"Based on what you said, the house will stand stable to the contrary. This is because the lumber is sure to bear weight with the mud to dry up to lighter weight, in which case the stronger the wood is going, the more likely it is to bear the weight of lighter mud due to evaporation of its water. Therefore, the mansion in construction won't come down," retorted the owner of the house.

Upon these words, the workers had no choice but to carry out the employer's instructions. In good form as the house was upon its completion, it broke apart shortly afterward. Gao Yangming, who has a sharp mind on minor affairs, is deficient in wisdom exerted on matters of paramount importance.

—— from *Spring and Autumn by Lv Buwei*

Application

As should be known, lessons drawn from professional advice or people's experience may bring us to the avoidance of making major mistakes in life or work. It is necessary that we conform to objective laws and respect experience coming from practice, which may equip us with knowledge of what end we may come to.

良狗捕鼠

齐有善相狗者，其邻假以买取鼠之狗。期年乃得之，曰："是良狗也。"其邻畜之数年而不取鼠，以告相者。相者曰："此良狗也。其志在獐麋豕鹿，不在鼠。欲其取鼠也则桎之。"其邻桎其后足，狗乃取鼠。夫骥骜之气，鸿鹄之志，有谕乎人心者，诚也。

——《吕氏春秋》

警 言

有了人才若不善用，就无法发挥他们的作用。善于用人，是上位者的眼光，也是其豁达的胸襟。于人如此，于物也如此。在生活中能够物尽其用，不仅避免了浪费，也体现了物主的眼光和智慧。

A Good Dog Kept to Catch the Rat

A man from the state of Qi was a good judge of dogs, who was capable of telling if it was a good dog or not. Once one of the man's neighbours trusted him to the matter of buying a dog to catch rats. Not until an entire year passed, did the man manage to find one for his neighbour.

"It's a good dog," said the judge of dogs.

Thereafter, the neighbour kept the dog for a number of years, which but never captured a rat. He informed the judge of all this.

"This is a good dog," explained the judge of dogs. "However, it yearns to hunt for the doe and the boar rather than the rat."

"If you want it to catch the rat, just bind its hind legs," the judge expounded further.

In compliance with his instructions, the neighbour tied up the dog's hind legs afterward, which led the animal to the rat chase. It is on account of the distinct temperament and aspiration that the gallant steed and the swan are known to all. It is true of man.

—— from *Spring and Autumn by Lv Buwei*

Application

If we know not to cast a talent in the right role, he won't be able to play their role to the proper extent. Knowing the appropriate role for a certain person is how the eye and the open mind of those in high positions are embodied. It is true of the object. Good use of objects to be made in life helps avoid a waste of money, reflecting the object owner's taste and wisdom.

炳烛而学

晋平公问于师旷曰:"吾年七十,欲学。恐已暮矣。"师旷曰:"何不炳烛乎?"平公曰:"安有为人臣而戏其君乎?"师旷曰:"盲臣安敢戏其君乎?臣闻之,少而好学,如日出之阳;壮而好学,如日中之光;老而好学,如炳烛之明。炳烛之明,孰与昧行乎?"平公曰:"善哉!"

——《说苑》

警言

学习如同点燃的蜡烛,虽然光亮有限,但也好过在黑暗中摸索。这则故事告诉我们,学无止境,不论年龄,都应保持学习的状态。

To Learn by Candlelight

"I am already in my seventies and I am desirous of learning. Is it too late?" King Ping of Jin consulted Shi Kuang.

"As it's late, why don't you light the candle?" responded Shi Kuang.

"How come an official is kidding his king?" raged the king.

"How dare I?" rejoined Shi Kuang. "As is said, learning in youth produces light that brightens like the rising sun, learning in the prime of life gives out light that shines like the midday sun, learning at the late age lets out light that glows like the candlelight. To walk in the dark or to walk in the candlelight, which is better?"

"What you said is good indeed," agreed the king.

——from *The Garden of Anecdotes*

Application

Learning like a lit candle may bring about confined light, which is better than the dark where one has to feel one's way. This fable warns us that it is never too late to learn though learning may bring forth light that but lights a small area.

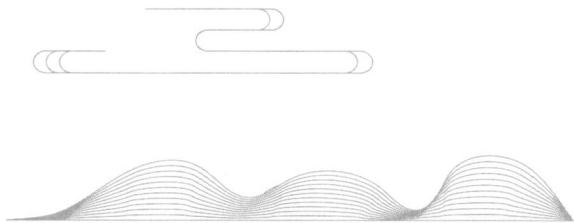

螳螂捕蝉，黄雀在后

园中有树，其上有蝉。蝉高居悲鸣饮露，不知螳螂在其后也；螳螂委身曲附欲取蝉，而不知黄雀茌其傍也；黄雀延颈啄螳螂，而不知弹丸在其下也。此三者，皆务欲得其前利，而不顾其后之有患也。

——《说苑》

警 言

这个故事启示我们，做事情要深思熟虑，避免只看眼前利益而忽略身后可能出现的危机或不良后果。

The Cicada, the Mantis and the Sparrow

In the garden stands a tree, in which is a cicada. This insect perches up therein, chirping and drinking the dew, not aware at all that a mantis is just behind him, stalking his prey. The Mantis humps up his back and leans his forelegs forward, ready to spring upon the Cicada, insensible of a sparrow beside it, in pursuit of his meal. The Sparrow, a hunter himself, cranes his neck to peck at the preying mantis, not knowing that a catapult has been set with a stone aimed at him somewhere below. All of the three gaze their eyes upon what has been laid in front of him, regardless of the latent perils that follow behind.

——from *The Garden of Anecdotes*

Application

This fable inspires us to be meticulous about pursuit of our desired interest in that it is somehow followed by some hidden risks or traps we are not aware of yet. Careful measurement of pros and cons, or profits to get and possible effects that come after may prevent us from a fall into abyss to the greatest extent.

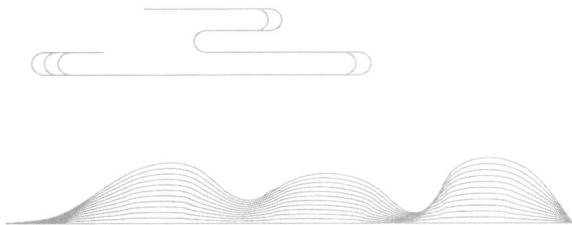

枭之东徙

　　枭逢鸠，鸠曰："子将安之？"枭曰："我将东徙。"鸠曰："何故？"枭曰："乡人皆恶我鸣，以故东徙。"鸠曰："子能更鸣可矣。不能更鸣，东徙，犹恶子之声。"

——《说苑》

警言

　　当遇到外界的指责时，不要盲目抱怨外界因素，而是应该从自身找原因，正视自己的缺点和错误，否则还会遇到同样的问题。

The Owl Moves House

One day the owl comes across the turtle-dove.

"Where are you heading?" enquires the turtle-dove.

"I'm moving east," replies the owl.

"Why are you moving east?" follows the turtle-dove's another question.

"All the villagers detest my hoot," the owl specifies, "and that's why I resolve to move to the east of the village."

"On the condition that you have any chance of making a change to your hoot," the turtle-dove says, "it's all right to move there. However, with no possibility of altering your voice, the people living in the east part will still loathe you for your unchanged way of crying."

—from *The Garden of Anecdotes*

Application

When you are somehow rebuked, do not lay blame on the one who brings the rebuke to you. In a bid to settle the problem, you are supposed to exert introspection, seeking out what is wrong with yourself. Otherwise, the same problem would repeat itself.

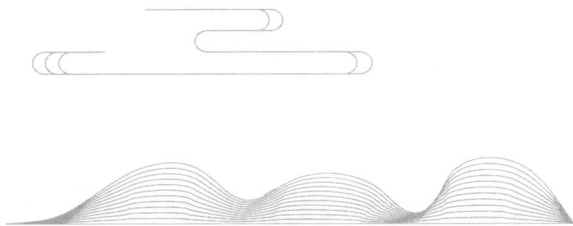

龙王变鱼

　　昔白龙下清冷之渊，化为鱼，渔者豫且射中其目。白龙上诉天帝，天帝曰："当是之时，若安置而形？"白龙对曰："我下清冷之渊，化为鱼。"天帝曰："鱼固人之所射已，若是，豫且何罪？"

——《说苑》

警 言

　　人在什么职位便应谋其相应的差，所在的位置决定了遇到的人，以及别人对你的态度和行为方式。人居于低位，则应承担低位所予的义务。居于低位，则不妄言居于高位时的光鲜。

The Dragon in the Form of a Fish

Once upon a time, a white dragon descended from heaven into a cool lake, taking the form of a fish. A fisherman, named Yu, shot him in the eye, which brought him to wild rage. The white dragon thereupon sued him to the Emperor of Heaven for this.

"What form did you take when you were shot?" queried the Emperor.

"I played there in the form of a fish," responded the dragon.

"A fish! That's what a fisherman seeks to shoot. In that case, what can you charge him with?" the Emperor of Heaven asked.

——from *The Garden of Anecdotes*

Application

You should run errands that your posts let you, which lead you to what kind of people you are to meet either in the working place or even in everyday life, and to how you are treated. Given that you are in a lower position, you should be subjected to your must-dos, either at the superiors' order or out of your sense of inferiority, in which case, you are not supposed to pride yourself on the superiority you enjoyed in the past or will have in the days ahead.

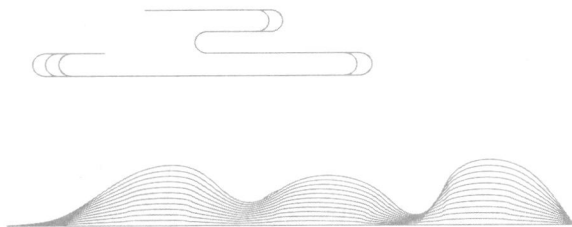

曾参杀人

　　昔者曾子处费，费人有与曾子同名族者而杀人，人告曾子母曰：“曾参杀人。”曾子之母曰：“吾子不杀人。”织自若。有顷焉，人又曰：“曾参杀人。”其母尚织自若也。顷之，一人又告之曰：“曾参杀人。”其母惧，投杼逾墙而走。

——《战国策》

警 言

　　这则寓言说明当负面信息大量涌来时，即便是最接近故事真相的人也会对真相产生怀疑。因此，这个故事警示人们在面对流言时，须保持理性，谨慎对待，通过求正而获得真相。

The Rumour that Zeng Tzu Committed Murder

Once upon a time, Zeng Tzu was at the town of Fei, where a man with the same name committed murder. Someone went to Zeng Tzu's mother with the story.

"Zeng Shen has killed a man," he told Zeng Tzu's mother.

"Nonsense," she responded, assured. "My son wouldn't kill."

With these words, she went on with her weaving, composed. After a while, someone else came to tell her the same thing.

"Zeng Shen has killed a man," said the messenger.

In spite of the news, Zeng Tzu's mother remained assertive, weaving. Some time later, a third man came with the same story.

"Zeng Shen has killed a man," stated the third man.

When someone drove home the news a third time, she got into considerable fright. Dropping the shuttle, she got away over the wall.

——from *Warring States Anecdotes*

Application

This fable intimates that as unfavourable news flooded to one from all sides, the one whoever is closest to the truth may cast doubts. Therefore, it warns us that we should stay rational, meticulous and investigative to seek for the truth.

鹬蚌相争

　　蚌方出曝,而鹬啄其肉。蚌合而拑其喙。鹬曰:"今日不雨,明日不雨,既有死蚌!"蚌亦谓鹬曰:"今日不出,明日不出,既有死鹬。"两者不肯相舍,渔者得而并禽之。

——《战国策》

警 言

　　两相争执,必会造成两败俱伤而第三方得利的局面。因此,在处理复杂的矛盾斗争时,应避免争执,避免因小失大。

The Snipe and the Clam

A clam leaves its shell open, basking in the warm sunshine, when a snipe comes to peck at its soft substance wrapped in the shell. The clam thereupon has the bird's beak clamped between its shells.

"If it doesn't rain today and tomorrow," the snipe claims, smug, "there will be a dead clam here."

"If you don't break loose today and tomorrow," the clam retorts in the like fashion, "there will be a dead snipe here."

As neither wins a concession from the other, a fisherman who happens to see this captures them both.

——from *Warring States Anecdotes*

Application

As two parties are in combat, loss will occur to both sides, which is in the most likelihood to the benefit of a third party uninvolved in the fight. Therefore, in collision with your opposing party, anything is worth trying to avoid conflict to save the risk of a larger loss.

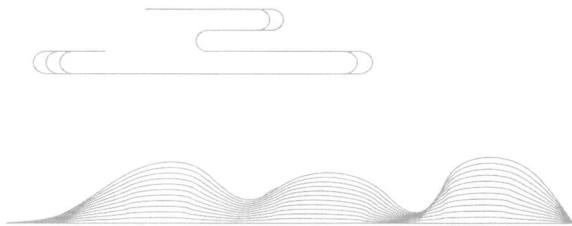

狐假虎威

虎求百兽而食之,得狐。狐曰:"子无敢食我也。天帝使我长百兽,今子食我,是逆天帝命也。子以我为不信,吾为子先行,子随我后,观百兽之见我而敢不走乎?"虎以为然,故遂与之行。兽见之皆走。虎不知兽畏己而走也,以为畏狐也。

—— 《战国策》

警 言

借助他人的威势来夸大自己的力量,往往会得到更多的关注和尊重,然而这只是虚张声势,一旦其实力和价值被揭穿,则会被打回原形。只有真正的才能和力量才会赢得众人的敬畏。

The Fox in the Exertion of the Tiger's Power

A tiger, when he was prowling in quest of prey, caught a fox.

"How dare you!" the fox bluffed. "The Emperor of Heaven has appointed me king of the beasts. If you eat me, you are against the decree he issued. If you don't believe my words, I'll precede you into the forest. As you'll see, whoever won't run away at the sight of me!"

Convinced of what the fox said, the tiger then strode along in company. Viewing the fox followed by the tiger, the beasts dashed away into the deep woods. The tiger, who was unaware that they fled in awe of himself, wrongly perceived that it was the fox they came across that was to the fright of the beasts.

——from *Warring States Anecdotes*

Application

With borrowed power to make oneself look stronger, one is liable to win more attention and respect. However, once a bluff is somehow identified, the truth is exposed to the mortal world where all your genuine value and power have no way to appear in a magnified disguise. Equipped with only real capacity and power, one may have more occasion to be led to distinction as well as grace.

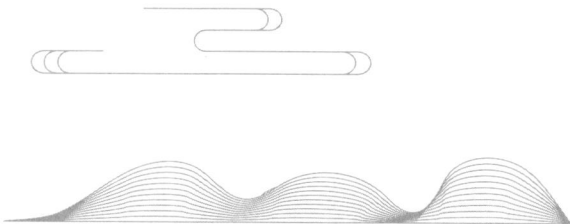

南辕北辙

魏王欲攻邯郸。季梁闻之，中道而反，衣焦不申，头尘不浴，往见王曰："今者臣来，见人于大行，方北面而持其驾，告臣曰：'我欲之楚。'臣曰：'君之楚，将奚为北面？'曰：'吾马良。'臣曰：'马虽良，此非楚之路也。'曰：'吾用多。'臣曰：'用虽多，此非楚之路也。'曰：'吾御者善。'此数者愈善，而离楚愈远耳！"

—— 《战国策》

警言

高尚的目标须配以正确方向的行动，方能抵达终点。无论做任何事，须先看准方向，才能最大限度地利用自己的有利条件；倘若方向错了，那么具备再有利的条件也枉然，只会与目标渐行渐远。

Heading North for Destination in the South

King of the state of Wei resolved to mount an attack upon Handan, capital of Zhao. Having heard this, Ji Liang turned around to the king midway, garments crumpled and head not dusted down.

"On my way back," he reported, "I ran across a man at the Taihang Mountain, who was driving his carriage northward. 'I'm going on my way to the state of Chu,' said he.

"'Now that your destination is Chu, why are you heading north?' wondered I.

"'That's all right,' he insisted assuredly. 'I have good horses.'

"'However good your horses are, you are going in the wrong direction,' as my response went.

"'The money on me is more than enough to cover my expenses on the way,' he went on.

"'With sufficient expenses though,' I specified, 'this is not the way to Chu.'

"'I have a skillful coachman,' he continued.

"'The better equipped you are, the sooner you'll get far from the state of Chu!'"

——from *Warring States Anecdotes*

Application

To reach a lofty destination, you need to go and act in the right direction. No matter what you aim at, you need to be correctly directed before you are able to take advantage of your strength to the full. If wrongly directed, you will run counter to your destination, with favourable equipment in vain.

画蛇添足

楚有祠者，赐其舍人卮酒，舍人相谓曰："数人饮之不足，一人饮之有余。请画地为蛇，先成者饮酒。"一人蛇先成，引酒且饮之，乃左手持卮，右手画蛇，曰："吾能为之足。"未成，一人之蛇成，夺其卮曰："蛇固无足，子安得为之足？"遂饮其酒。为蛇足者，终亡其酒。

——《战国策》

警言

做任何事，最重要的是恰到好处，做得太多有时还不如不做，所谓过犹不及。不懂得把握分寸，则会弄巧成拙，把好事办坏，得不偿失。

Drawing a Snake with Added Legs

In the state of Chu, a man held a sacrifice for ancestor worship, during which he offered a cup of wine to his men that were in the role of counselor and follower.

"It won't suffice for all," they discussed, "but for more than one. Let's draw the snake on the ground, and the first one to finish drawing will have the wine."

One of them, who completed drawing first, took the cup, ready to drink. However, holding it in his left hand, he kept drawing with his right. "I can have even time for the legs," he boasted.

Before the legs were added, another one of them finished his snake and grabbed the cup from the earlier one, "A snake has no legs," criticized the latter drawer. "Why add legs to the snake?" With these words, he then drained the wine in one gulp.

Thereupon, the one who drew the snake with added legs lost the chance of touching the cup.

——from *Warring States Anecdotes*

Application

It is more important to do something appropriately than to do it overly. Going too far is as good as inadequate or insufficient, as the Chinese saying goes. Therefore, have the sense of propriety, which helps avoid transforming a good deal into a bad one, thus leading to a joyous gain rather than a pathetic loss.

邹忌比美

邹忌修八尺有余，身体昳丽。朝服衣冠，窥镜，谓其妻曰："我孰与城北徐公美？"其妻曰："君美甚。徐公何能及君也！"城北徐公，齐国之美丽者也。忌不自信，而复问其妾曰："吾孰与徐公美？"妾曰："徐公何能及君也！"旦日，客从外来，与坐谈，问之客曰："吾与徐公孰美？"客曰："徐公不若君之美也！"明日，徐公来。孰视之，自以为不如；窥镜而自视，又弗如远甚。暮寝而思之，曰："吾妻之美我者，私我也！妾之美我者，畏我也！客之美我者，欲有求于我也！"

——《战国策》

警言

要避免主观臆断，不盲目自信，要善于分析、善于反思、保持头脑清醒、实事求是、有自知之明，才能看到事物的本质。

Which One Is More Handsome?

Lord Zou Ji, over six feet tall, has a good-looking face as well as a masculine figure. As he got dressed one morning, he scrutinized himself in the mirror.

"Which one is more handsome," he posed a question to his wife, "Lord Xu living in the north town or I?"

"You are so very handsome," replied his wife. "How can Lord Xu compare with you?"

Lord Xu in the north of the town was recognized for his good looks throughout the sate of Qi. Zou Ji did not assure himself of his wife's admiring words, which brought him to a repetition of the same question to his concubine.

"How can Lord Xu compare with you?" exclaimed his concubine.

The following day came a protege, with whom Zou Ji was conversing and who then was asked the same question.

"Lord Xu is not so good-looking as Your Excellency is," was the reply.

The day after that, Lord Xu himself came for a visit. With a thorough scrutiny, Zou Ji decided that he was by no means so handsome as Lord Xu. As he looked at himself in the mirror, he concluded that he was far less handsome than Lord Xu. That very night he contemplated this in bed with a conclusion, "My wife said I was the more handsome of the two due to her love for me; my concubine said so owing to her awe of me; and my protege said so thanks to the favours to ask from me."

——from *Warring States Anecdotes*

Application

Biased judgments and undue self-assurance are a bar to access to the essence of what you are faced with or what's going on. A combination of impartial analysis, self reflection and sobriety leads to an enhanced understanding of the earthly world as well as the beings in it.

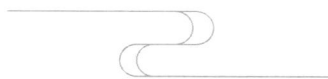

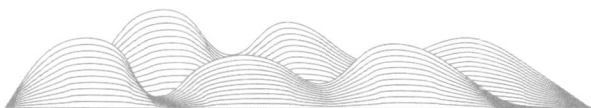

泥人和木偶

孟尝君将入秦，止者千数而弗听。苏秦欲止之。孟尝曰："人事者，吾已尽知之矣；吾所未闻者，独鬼事耳。"苏秦曰："臣之来也，固不取言人事也，固且以鬼事相见君。"

孟尝君见之。谓孟尝君曰："今者臣来，过于淄上，有土偶人与桃梗相与语。桃梗谓土偶人曰：'子，西岸之土也，埏子以为人，至岁八月，降雨下，淄水至，则汝残矣。'土偶曰：'不然。吾西岸之土也，吾残则复西岸耳。今子，东国之桃梗也，刻削子之为人，降雨下，淄水至，流子而去，则子漂漂者将何如耳。'今秦，四塞之国，譬若虎口，而君入之，则臣不知君所出矣。"孟尝君乃止。

——《战国策》

任何人都有缺点，勿要只看到他人的不足而自觉高人一等，在嘲笑别人的缺点之前，不妨先反思一下自身。因此，保持谦虚、不骄不躁，才能不断进步，且更快进步。

The Clay Figure and the Wooden Image

When Lord Mengchang, whose native land was the state of Qi, resolved on taking office in the state of Qin, hundreds of men tried to dissuade him from being an official there, so did Su Qin.

"I have had a thorough knowledge of the worldly happenings," said Lord Mengchang. "Out of my knowledge is what is supernaturally involved."

"I came to you not to involve you in affairs of the mortals," explained Su Qin, "but to discuss about the phantoms and monsters."

Admitted in by the lord, Su Qin stated, "Passing the Zi River on my way over here, I overheard a conversation between a clay figure and a peach-wood image."

"'You used to be a lump of clay on the west bank,' said the wooden image. 'Shaped into a figure, you are bound to be destroyed as the river rises during the rains in the eighth moon.'

"'What of it?' argued the clay figure. 'Coming from the west bank, I will be restored to where I am from. However, you were a piece of peach wood transported from the eastern land, carved by the craftsman into an image. As the rains come, the river rises, sweeping you away. By then, where on earth are you going afloat?'

"With the state of Qin enclosed by strong fortresses on all sides, you will enter a tiger's mouth once you get in and I have no idea whether you will come out of it safe and sound."

Upon these words of the great rhetorician of Su Qin, Lord Mengchang ceased his plan.

——from *Warring States Anecdotes*

Application

Each and every one in the world that has his weaknesses or defects is supposed to reflect on himself, with considerable occasion to overlook weaknesses of one's own. Therefore, a gesture of modesty may to a large extent keep one struggling forward.

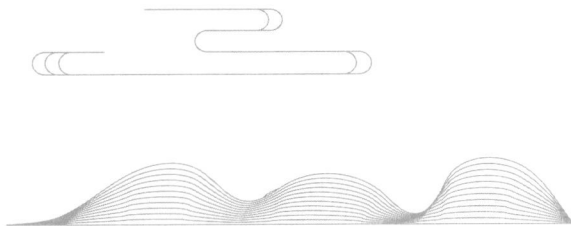

亡羊补牢

庄辛至,襄王曰:"寡人不能用先生之言,今事至于此,为之奈何?"庄辛对曰:"臣闻鄙语曰:'见兔而顾犬,未为晚也;亡羊而补牢,未为迟也。'臣闻昔汤、武以百里昌,桀、纣以天下亡。今楚国虽小,绝长续短,犹以数千里,岂特百里哉!"

——《战国策》

警 言

在生活中或工作中,出现问题后,应及时采取补救措施,以避免遭受更大的损失。若在发现了错误时,未能及时止损,待时间过久则失去了补救的机会。

Not Too Late to Mend the Fold When a Sheep Is Lost

Zhuang Xin, minister of Chu, made his return to the land of Chu.

"I'm sorry that I failed to pay heed to your suggestions," said King Xiang of Chu to Zhuang Xin. "As things have come to this point, what can be done with it?"

"As the saying goes, 'It's never too late to let go the hound when you sight the hare and it's not late to mend the fold when you've found a sheep is lost,'" stated Zhuang Xin. "I hear that Tang of Shang Dynasty and King Wu of Zhou Dynasty flourished up based on a country with a small area of round a hundred square *li* while Jie of Xia and Zhou of Shang who ever ruled over the land known to exist perished in the end. Small as the state of Chu remains, more or less, we have a circumference of a thousand *li*, far greater than a hundred *li*."

——from *Warring States Anecdotes*

Application

Whatever it is, at work or in everyday life, remedial measures ought to be referred to upon the emergence of issues or trouble to avoid greater losses. Given a slip or error found out but not disposed of, a small loss may lead to a tremendous one on account of little resort to any remedy to prevent the situation from deteriorating. Thereupon we can't take chance to exert remedial steps in an enduring length of time.

惊弓之鸟

异日者，更羸与魏王处京台之下，仰见飞鸟。更羸谓魏王曰："臣为王引弓虚发而下鸟。"魏王曰："然则射可至此乎？"更羸曰："可。"有间，雁从东方来，更羸以虚发而下之。魏王曰："然则射可至此乎？"更羸曰："此孽也。"王曰："先生何以知之？对曰："其飞徐而鸣悲。飞徐者，故疮痛也；鸣悲者，久失群也。故疮未息而惊心未忘也。闻弦音，引而高飞，故疮裂而陨也。"

—— 《战国策》

警言

这则寓言说明了观察的力量。基于细心的观察，才能进行准确的分析和判断。任何技巧的诉诸 均来自对内在本质的洞悉，而这种洞悉则生成于细致的观察。

A Bird Surprised Down by the Arrow

Once Geng Lei and the king of Wei, standing somewhere near the lookout, looked up to the sky and saw a bird soaring past. At this moment, the former volunteered to bring the bird down.

"I venture to let the bird down for Your Majesty with an empty bow to pull," the former offered.

"Has the art of shooting gone as marvellous as this?" wondered the king.

"Yes, Your Majesty," responded the archer.

Shortly afterward, the bird flew over from the east, when Geng Lei surprised the bird with a slight pluck of his bow, which whooshed all the way down from in the air.

"Has the art of shooting gone as marvellous as this?" enquired the king, amazed.

"It's because the bird has an unhealed wound," replied the archer.

"How did you know of it?" marvelled the king.

"It flew slowly and cried sadly," answered the archer. "It flew slowly because the unhealed wound led to pain and it cried sadly because it had fallen out of its flock a long time before."

"With its old wound unhealed, the bird remained panic-stricken," specified the archer. "Hearing the pluck of the bow, it struggled upward in the air only to make its old wound split. Then it came down."

——from *Warring States Anecdotes*

Application

This fable indicates the power of observation, on which analysis and judgment are based, bringing along accuracy and reliability. Any resort to a technique arises from insight into the nature or essence, which in turn descends from meticulous practice of observation

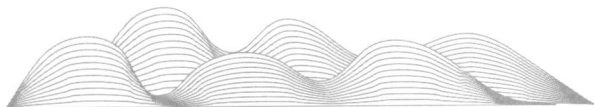

千金买马首

古之人君,有以千金求千里马者,三年不能得。涓人言于君曰:"请求之。"君遣之。三月得千里马,马已死,买其首五百金,反以报君。君大怒曰:"所求者生马,安事死马而捐五百金?"涓人对曰:"死马且买之五百金,况生马乎?天下必以王为能市马,马今至矣。"于是不能期年,千里之马至者三。

——《战国策》

警 言

招揽人才,除了以足够大的利益去吸引其之外,还要以实际行动表现出渴慕人才的真心实意,这样方能激励人才加入。

Buying a Horse's Skull with a Thousand Taels of Gold

Once upon a time, there lived a king who wished for a horse that could run a thousand *li* nonstop at a thousand taels of gold for a prolonged period of three years, but in vain.

"May I venture to seek for one for you, Your Majesty?" one of the king's attendants offered.

To his offer the king agreed. Three months later, this errand-runner brought back to the king a skull of a horse that could run a thousand *li* nonstop, on which he spent five hundred taels of gold. The king was infuriated by this.

"I sent you for a live horse!" the king barked out. "How come you wasted five hundred pieces of gold on a dead horse?"

"A dead horse is worth five hundred pieces of gold, let alone a live one," explained the attendant. "Once the news spreads, people will know you are disposed to buy good horses, which will lead more good horses to Your Majesty."

Thereafter, it was in less than a year that the king held in possession three extraordinary horses.

——from *Warring States Anecdotes*

Application

To recruit talents, besides sufficient interest to draw those of talent, actions are required to represent the genuine desire to yearn for talents. Only by this means, will people of competence join a team or company.

羊蒙虎皮

羊质而虎皮,见草而说,见豺而战,忘其皮之虎矣。

——《法言》

警 言

外表的强大弥补不了内在的弱小。强大的外表只能是自欺欺人,而内在的空虚在遇到检验实力的时候还是会让这个自欺欺人的人内心胆怯。这告诉我们,没有强大的实力就不要进行虚伪的伪装,这种伪装迟早会被揭穿。这还告诉我们,要善于透过现象看本质,若遇到一个如此的对手,不要被其强大的表象所压倒,只要你真正有实力,总能够战胜虎皮下的羔羊。

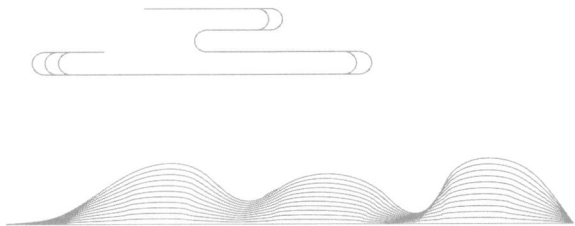

The Lamb in a Tiger's Skin

A lamb chanced to clothe himself in a tiger's skin as a disguise. The lamb that masqueraded as a tiger got overwhelmed with elation at the sight of green grass while a wolf in his sight would send him shuddering from head to tail. In the actual fact, the lamb failed to bear it in mind that he was camouflaged as a tiger.

——from *Judgments on Rights and Wrongs*

Application

No matter how invincible we seem on the surface, there is no chance of seeming invincibility being a compensation for the inner weakness. Fake invincibility, relieving ourselves of the sense of deficiency, cannot save us from the sense of timidity in the face of power test. This fable warns us not to behave in masquerade, which will be sooner or later unmasked to all. Plus, it advises us to see through what is in sight into what is inside. When we have a like opponent, we need to know not to be overwhelmed by their power-bearing appearances; for as long as you are capable enough, you must be able to defeat the tiger-skinned lamb.

哭　母

　　东家母死,其子哭之不哀。西家子见之,归谓其母曰:"社何爱速死? 吾必悲哭社。"

　　夫欲其母之死者,虽死亦不能悲哭矣。

——《淮南子》

警　言

　　不想让母亲死去的人,母逝而子哭;想让母亲死的人,纵使母亲真的死了,也不可能感到悲伤而痛哭。

Crying for Mother's Death

The man, who lived in the east of town and whose mother passed away, cried a loud cry for the deceased with no grief. A man living in the west of town saw this, went home and said to his mother, "Why won't you die soon? In this case, I'm sure to wail badly."

Given that his mother was gone, he, who was desirous of her death, was unlikely to wail in grief over her.

——from *Huainan Tzu*

Application

He who is not desirous of his mother's death will wail in grief if his mother passes away. He who is desirous of his mother's death won't grieve, crying, even if his mother is gone.

盲人和跛子

寇难至，躄者告盲者，盲者负而走，两人皆活。得其所能也。故使盲者语，使躄者走，失其所也。

——《淮南子》

警 言

世间的每个人都像是盲人或跛子，都有自身的缺点，往往需要其他人的帮助。因此，在生活中，我们要学会取长补短，培养协作意识，发挥自身的长处，以达成共同的目标。

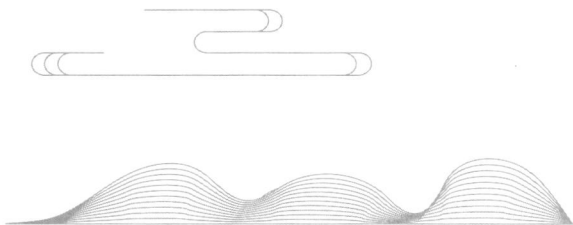

A Blind Man and a Lame Man

The country was invaded by its enemy troops, of which a lame man informed a blind man. The blind one fled thereupon, carrying the lame one on his back, the two of whom both survived the war then. They made it because one informed the other who lent legs to the messenger, their respective strength combinedly brought into play. Provided that the blind man was made the messenger and the lame one to carry the blind, either of them would be deprived of his own strength.

——from *Huainan Tzu*

Application

Every one of us in this mortal world was born with a certain defect, say blind or lame, calling for help from others who are equipped with something that proved to be a deficiency of another one. Under this circumstance, we should have the sense of cooperation, employing each other's strengths to offset our own weaknesses, with our own strong points in active use, in order to achieve the two parties' shared goal.

塞翁失马

　　近塞上之人，有善术者，马无故亡而入胡。人皆吊之。其父曰："此何遽不为福乎？"居数月，其马将胡骏马而归。人皆贺之。其父曰："此何遽不能为祸乎？"家富良马，其子好骑，堕而折其髀，人皆吊之，其父曰："此何遽不为福乎？"居一年，胡人大入塞，丁壮者引弦而战。近塞之人，死者十九，此独以跛之故，父子相保。

　　　　　　　　　　　　　　　　　　　　——《淮南子》

警　言

　　祸兮福所倚，福兮祸所伏。任何事都具有两面性，目前看起来不好的可能向好的方面转化，目前看起来好的也可能向坏的结果发展。因此，保持积极、乐观以及豁达的心态非常重要。

An Old Man Living at the Frontier Losing His Horse

At the frontier in the proximity of the Huns lived an old man pursuing divination, whose horse once lost his way somehow into the Huns' territory. Neighbours came to him to convey their kindness of comfort, but the old diviner remarked, "Why isn't it a good thing?" A few months passed before the lost horse returned, followed by some Huns' horses. People living about came to him to congratulate the family on that, but the man said, "Why can't it be a bad thing?" Having good horses, the diviner had a son, who, fond of horseriding, fell off the horse to a fracture of the leg. Like before, those who lived nearby came again to show sympathy for the man's son for what had happened to his leg, but the man commented, "Why isn't t a good thing?" After a year, the Huns encroached upon the frontier in large troops, which brought all young grown-up men to the bows and arrows for the war. Those who lived around the frontier, for the most part, died a soldier's death. Only the man's son averted the chance of losing his life in battles on account of his being crippled, both lives of the father and the son then sustained to and beyond the end of the war.

——from *Huainan Tzu*

Application

A good thing oftentimes comes behind a bad one and a bad thing ensues after a good one, the two of which are most likely to run counter to each other. Every coin has two sides. What seems undesirable may develop in the direction of what you aspire to while what looks agreeable on the surface may advance to what you to the largest degree reject. Therefore, a positive attitude and optimism and a broad heart may take occasion to release you of unnamable burdens in life, thus a self-assured life to be had.

对牛弹琴

公明仪为牛弹清角之操，伏食如故。非牛不闻，不合其耳矣。转为蚊虻之声、孤犊之鸣，即掉尾、奋耳，蹀躞而听。

——《牟子》

警 言

与愚蠢的人谈论高深的道理，等于白费口舌。这则故事告诫人们，办事说话要看对象；教育也要看对象，因材施教。

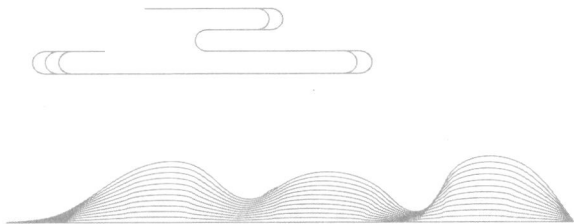

Playing Guqin to a Cow

The celebrated musician of Gongming Yi was playing a melodious tune on guqin, a seven-stringed plucked instrument similar to a zither, to a cow, which kept browsing, chomping on grass as usual with no heed given to the music at all. It wasn't that the cow did not attend to the tune, which but did not cater to his taste. Therefore, he plucked the strings for different notes to change into drones of mosquitoes and buzzes of gadflies and bleats of calves, which led to the cow flicking its tail, pricking up its ears, and capering around.

——from *Mou Tzu*

Application

To argue about something profound with someone whose comprehension is very limited, to a large extent, comes to no fruit. This fable warns us to attend to who we are connecting with, thus adopting specific means for communication.

杯弓蛇影

予之祖父郴,为汲令,以夏至日诣见主簿杜宣,赐酒。时北壁上有悬赤弩,照于杯,形如蛇,宣畏恶之,然不敢不饮。其日,便得胸腹痛切,妨损饮食,大用羸露,攻治万端,不为愈。后郴因事过至宣家,窥视,问其变故。云:"畏此蛇,蛇入腹中。"郴还听事,思惟良久,顾见悬弩,必是也。则使门下史将铃下侍,徐扶辇载宣,于故处设酒,杯中故复有蛇,因谓宣:"此壁上弩影耳,非有他怪。"宣遂解,甚夷怿,由是瘳平。

——《风俗通义》

警 言

做事情要心胸坦荡,不要没有根据地疑神疑鬼。另外,遇到问题时,也要善于思考,不要被事情的假象所迷惑。

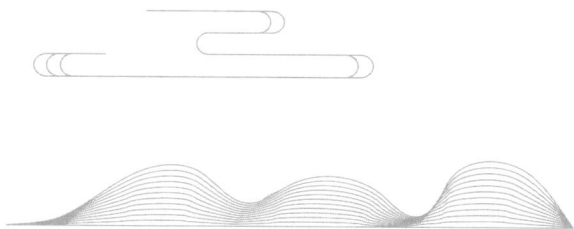

The Snaky Shadow of the Bow in the Cup

My grandfather, magistrate of the county of Ji, invited Du Xuan, deputy magistrate, to his home, treating him to a drink on summer solstice. At that time, a red bow that hung on the north wall cast a snake-shaped shadow in the cup. Frightened though he was, Du Xuan did not dare to refuse to drain it when asked to. Later that very day, he felt a severe stomachache, which led to little diet and increasing frailty for a continued period of time. All manner of prescribed drugs tried, he was not cured, however.

Some time afterward, my grandfather called on him for business to find him ill, who then enquired how he had contracted the disease.

"It's because of the snake that I swallowed," replied Du Xuan.

So bewildered was my grandfather by Du Xuan's words. Upon coming back to his lounge, my grandfather reflected on this for a long time before he turned around, his eyes laid on the bow. With the arch into his sight, it struck him that "the snake" must be the bow. He sent his subordinate to escort Du Xuan over to his house in a carriage. With wine cups set at the same place, in the cup came a snake once more.

"It's no more than a shadow of the bow on the wall," explained my grandfather.

Realizing what it truly was, Du Xuan, whose heart lifted, got completely healed of the pain in the stomach as well as the fear.

——from *General Traditions and Customs*

Application

Suspicion that comes on no grounds suggests an unclear conscience, any kind of which should be brought to clarification. This way, it won't consume much of your time and energy, giving rise to anxiety or even a severe disease. From a different perspective, using our head, we should avoid any confused reflection.

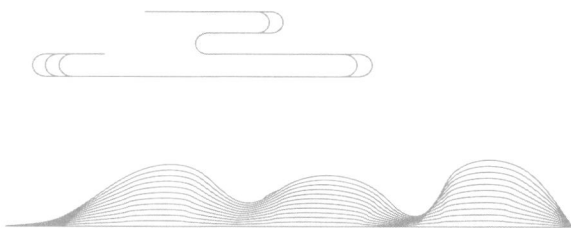

两只眼睛

　　昔有二人共评主者。一人曰"好。"一人曰:"丑。"久而不决。二人各曰:"尔可求人,吾目中则妍丑分矣。"士有定形,二人察之有得失,非苟相反,眼睛异耳。

——《万机论》

警言

　　人对同一事物的看法往往因角度、立场、所处环境以及审美的不同而具有差异。所谓眼光,除涉及以上提到的因素,还涉及教养、性格等诸多其他因素。

Two Eyes

Two men discussed the monarch, with the focus on his appearance.

"Handsome!" commented one.

"Ugly!" disagreed the other.

Their discussion lasted a prolonged time for no conclusion to be reached. In this circumstance, each said to the other, "Let's get a third party to remark on which of us is right."

Those, who look at whatever or whoever has fixed features, hold remarkably different opinions. It is not because people deliberately oppose each other, but because each of them sees with a different eye.

——from *Miscellaneous Anecdotes*

Application

It is for the difference in perspectives from which to see things, like one's standpoint, conditions to be equipped with and an aesthetic appreciation that people hold varied viewpoints on the same subject. Beyond, the difference in education, family background, personality and so on may contribute to the rise of disagreement between people.

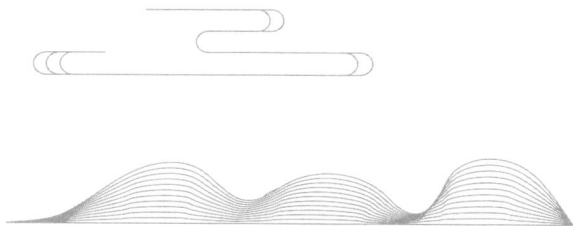

黔驴技穷

　　黔无驴，有好事者，船载以入；至则无可用，放之山下。虎视之，庞然大物也，以为神；蔽林间窥之，稍出近之，慭慭然，莫相知。他日，驴一鸣，虎大骇，远遁，以为且噬己也，甚恐；然往来视之，觉无异能者；益习其声，又近出前后，终不敢搏。稍近，益狎，荡倚冲冒，驴不胜怒，蹄之。虎因喜，计之曰"技止此耳！"因跳踉大㘎，断其喉，尽其肉，乃去。

——《柳河东集》

警言

　　貌似强大的敌人是否真的强大，要透过表象才能真正了解，要敢于斗争。换个角度说，一个人不能只靠虚张声势的外表，而应注重本领的学习和能力的培养，这样才不会在强敌来临之时任人蹂躏。

The Donkey and the Tiger

There existed no donkey in Guizhou until some guy intrigued by novelties brought one in by ship, who, found of no practical use, was thereby left free at the foot of the hill. The time the donkey leapt in a tiger's sight, the latter deemed the monstrous beast as divine, hiding behind trees and peeking through at him in the wood. Bit by bit the tiger ventured to edge up to a safety distance of the unnamable beast, with no knowledge of what exactly the beast was. One day, the donkey let out a clamourous bray, of which the tiger got horrified, retreating to a greater distance for fear of falling prey to him, struck by panic. Nevertheless, the tiger regained the donkey's demesne repeatedly before he decided that the eccentric beast was not that unbearably formidable. Shortly afterward, he grew accustomed to the donkey's unpleasant cries, and attempted his approach from all around without the daring to make at him though. Drawing nearer still, the native beast took liberty, shoving, jostling, and charging at the alien before the new comer sprang into rage, kicking at the native bully.

"All his tricks have been exhausted," thought the tiger in rapture.

With this calculation in his mind, the ferocious hunter pranced fiercely upon his prey in the disguise of a monster and his jaws closed upon the donkey's throat before he devoured the entire donkey and took off.

——from *Collected Works of Liu Zongyuan*

Application

It is a thorough scrutiny through the surface that allows you to know whether an opponent that looks strong and powerful is of real power or not. Therefore, brave strife! From a changed perspective, one cannot scare away a threat to him with his bluffing appearances, but he repels the threat with his power and ability, so that he won't need to be afflicted by any aggression.

猎人骗猎

鹿畏貙，貙畏虎，虎畏罴。罴之状，被发人立，绝有力而甚害人焉！

楚之南有猎者，能吹竹为百兽之音。昔云，持弓、矢、罂、火而即之山，为鹿鸣以感其类，伺其至，发火而射之。貙闻其鹿也，趋而至，其人恐，因为虎而骇之。貙走而虎至，愈恐，则又为罴，虎亦亡去。罴闻而求其类，至，则人也，捽搏挽裂而食之。

今夫不善内而恃外者，未有不为罴之食也！

——《柳河东集》

警 言

没有真才实学，只靠不断欺骗，最终将自食其果。

The Hunter and His Trick

The deer is in dread of the wolf by nature, the wolf of the tiger and the tiger of the wild bear. The bear walks upright like a man with his long hair down, most ferocious and liable to attack human beings.

In the south of Chu lived a hunter who could make the sounds of many an animal with a bamboo pipe. As said, he once took to the mountain with his bow, arrow, bottles and fire, where he let out a mimick of the deer cries to lure a herd of deer over and upon their arrival, he shot the entire herd with the fire-lit arrows. The wolf, led by the mimicked deer cries, came all the way to the hunter. This was to the hunter's fright, which inspired him to resort to the mimick of the roars of the tiger. Off went the wolf, but came a tiger. Overwhelmed with terror, the hunter gave out the cry of the bear, which scared away the tiger but brought a bear to the confused scene. Following the sound, the bear thought it was of its own kind and came for it, only to find it was a man. The large animal then seized upon him, tore him into several pieces, and devoured him up.

Those, with their attention unpaid to their inner strength development, resort in the most possibility to outer insubstantial tricks, which may bring them to a sorry end like that of the hunter's.

——from *Collected Works of Liu Zongyuan*

Application

You reap what you sow if you don't exert yourself in terms of inner power development. Any trick done is referred to as tricking the tricker himself.

临江之麋

临江之人，畋得麋麑，畜之。入门，群犬垂涎，扬尾皆来。其人怒怛之。自是日抱就犬，习示之，使勿动；稍使与之戏。积久，犬皆如人意。麋麑稍大，忘己之麋也，以为犬良我友，抵触偃仆，益狎。犬畏主人，与之俯仰甚善，然时啖其舌。

三年，麋出门，见外犬在道甚众，走欲与为戏。外犬见而喜且怒，共杀食之，狼藉道上。麋至死不悟。

——《柳河东集》

警 言

有一些小人物，依仗权贵而得意忘形、恃宠而骄，不知道自己所得的荣耀是建立在权贵相辅的基础上的，在脱离了外部保护的情况下，将走向悲惨的结局。

The Death of the Flattered Fawn

A hunter, who was from Linjiang, captured a fawn once and kept it at home afterward. As the fawn followed the man through the gate, the whole pack of his domesticated dogs coveted it as prey, wagging their tails. The master of the dogs shooed them off with menacing anger. From then on, the hunter let the little deer mix with the dogs, bade them stop their stir, and even made them frolic with it. Over a period of time, the dogs came to behave as the man required. As it grew older, the flattered fawn, who lost its recollection of what it was as well as a reserve of latent danger around, regarded the dogs as its friends, with whom it gamboled, turned somersaults back and forth, and thereby achieved more and more intimacy. The dogs, in awe of their master, flattered the hunter's favoured pet with the suppression of the call of the inner desire, fraternizing with it. However, they licked their chops from time to time where they went unnoticed.

Three years passed. One day, the deer went out in the street where many a dog came in sight. Cheerfully, it capered up to them for fraternal interaction. A little struck by the wonderful surprise, the street dogs were delighted to find a meal coming its way to them, threw themselves upon and sank their teeth into it. What a mess! The time it was nearing death, the young deer had little idea of why it met so tragic and untimely a death.

——from *Collected Works of Liu Zongyuan*

Application

Some nobody, who had a strong family influence or connections with power, is found complacent and haughty on account of his powerful background, unaware that his lofty status or priority is achieved through what his background equips him with. Therefore, once deprived of the backup, his life is coming to a tragedy.

伤仲永

　　金溪民方仲永，世隶耕。仲永生五年，未尝识书具，忽啼求之。父异焉，借旁近与之，即书诗四句，并自为其名。其诗以养父母、收族为意，传一乡秀才观之。自是指物作诗立就，其文理皆有可观者。邑人奇之，稍稍宾客其父，或以钱币乞之。父利其然也，日扳仲永还谒于邑人，不使学。

　　余闻之也久。明道中，从先人还家，于舅家见之，十二三矣。令作诗，不能称前时之闻。又七年，还自扬州，复到舅家问焉，曰："泯然众人矣。"

　　王子曰：仲永之通悟，受之天也。其受之天也，贤于材人远矣。卒之为众人，则其受于人者不至也。彼其受之天也，如此其贤也，不受之人，且为众人；今夫不受之天，固众人，又不受之人，得为众人而已耶？

——《临川先生文集》

警言

　　这则故事告诉我们，后天教育和学习是非常重要的。有天赋实乃幸事。然而，若仅仅依靠天资，吃老本，而不持续学习，就连本有的天资也会消耗殆尽，最终沦落为芸人。

The Story of Zhongyong

There lived a child by the name of Fang Zhongyong at the county of Jinxi, where his family farmed the land for a living from generation to generation. The child was never put to any knowledge of instruments used to write. Of a sudden, Zhongyong cried for these things one day. Much to his father's surprise though, he went to his neighbour, from whom he borrowed the writing brush, ink and so on, with which the boy wrote down a poem of four lines straight away, followed by his signature. The poem, themed on maintaining parents and rallying around clansmen, was presented to the scholars that had passed the county-level imperial exam. Once provided a designated theme, the boy was able to compose in no time a poem that commanded appreciation as regards the literary talent and the moral. People across the county marvelled at this, treating Zhongyong's father with due respect and some of them even asked for the child's poems in exchange with money. Elated by the prospect of the easy access to money, the father thereby led the son to daily visit to people all over the county rather than to lessons.

It had been long since I heard of the prodigy. Not until I went back to my hometown with my father in the period of King Mingdao, did I take occasion to meet the child prodigy of twelve or thirteen. I asked him to write a poem, but the one he made was not equal to his fame. Seven years passed. As I came back from Yangzhou to call on my uncle, I enquired as to Fang Zhongyong.

"He is an average person now," commented my uncle.

Fang Zhongyong's brightness bestowed by the Heaven, says Wang Anshi, his talent is far greater than that of ordinary talented people; it is because of his deficiency of education that he made a mediocre man; equipped with his superb endowments, he failed to receive a good education, which led to his mediocrity while those who are not so well equipped, without education, are subject to mediocrity, aren't they?

——from *Collected Works of Scholar Linchuan*

Application

This fable warns us that acquisition of knowledge is of great significance in the building of one's capability, which arises, for the most part, from education rather than aptitude. An aptitude is endowed by the Heaven and it is fortunate to have it. However, rest on one's endowments without persistent learning may lead to the exhaustion of his aptitude and even to mediocrity in the end.

龙王和青蛙

龙王逢一蛙于海滨，相问讯后，蛙问龙王曰："王之居何处如？"王曰："珠宫贝阙，翚非璇题。"龙复问："汝之居处何若？"蛙曰："绿苔碧草，清泉白石。"

复问曰："王之喜怒如何？"龙曰："吾喜则时降膏泽，使五谷丰稔；怒则先之以暴风，次之以震霆，继之以飞电，使千里之内寸草不留。"龙问蛙曰："汝之喜怒何如？"曰："吾之喜则清风明月，一部鼓吹；怒则先之以努眼，次之以腹胀，至于胀过而休。"

——《艾子杂说》

警言

世间百态，人各自有命。有能力做大事、起大作用的，便为国为民，能力小的便做好自己手边的事。对人对事没有必要强行使用同一标准，人的生活和理念也不必出自同一模式，能力大有大的意义，能力小有小的价值，这便是世间百态。

The Dragon King and the Frog

The Dragon King ran across the Frog by the lake. After they extended greetings to each other, the latter enquired, "What is your dwelling place like, Your Highness?"

"It's a palace built of pearls and seashells with upturned eaves and rafters inlayed with jade at both ends," replied the Dragon King.

"What is your dwelling place like?" he asked in return.

"It's a place by a clear spring and white stones, with green moss and grass that runs around its four sides," replied the Frog.

"What are your joy and rage like, Your Highness?" he asked again.

"When joyous, I will let it rain in a bid to have a good harvest to be had; when in rage, I will let the wind blow savagely, there be cracking thunders and flashes of lightning follow, which leads to loss of grass in the area of a thousand *li* in circumference," said the Dragon King. "What are yours like?"

"When I'm delighted, the breeze blows gentle and the moon shines bright with bursts upon bursts of melodious croaks," said the Frog smugly. "When I'm furious, my eyes bulge, my belly puffs up, and it puffs up until it reaches its maximum."

——from *Ai Tzu's Fables*

Application

The world, where every single being has his destined place, exists in a diversity of forms. Those of great power have the inclination for an important role, serving the country and the people while those of minor abilities commit themselves to trivial matters, which leads to the difference in making standards with which to measure and a distinction in life views and philosophy. Whether one's power is great or not, the existence of it, as part of the world, constructs the variety in which the world comes.

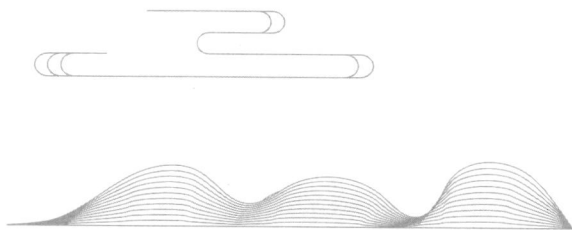

求鸭搦兔

昔人将猎而不识鹘，买一凫而去。原上兔起，掷之使击，凫不能飞。投于地，再掷之，又投于地，至三四。凫忽蹒跚而人语曰："我鸭也，杀而食之，乃其分，奈何加我以掷之苦乎？"其人曰："我谓尔为鹘，可以猎兔耳，乃鸭耶？"凫举掌而示，笑以言曰："看我这脚手，可以搦得兔否？"

——《艾子杂说》

要想更好地运用某种本领或者人的技能，必须首先清楚地了解其作用、运转的原理以及可能达到的效果。若不能，则无法达到预期的效果或作用。

Seeking a Duck to Capture the Hare

Once upon a time, there lived a man in search of a hawk for hunting. However, not knowing what a hawk was like, the man on the purchase brought home a duck, which he thought was a hawk and which he took along with him to the wild. From somewhere in the wild darted a hare. Throwing the duck in the air, the man meant to let the bird fly upon the hare and capture it. However, the duck that was unable to fly plunged onto the ground. He flung it in the air again, but it dropped onto the ground once more. After he repeated the throw a third and fourth time, the duck, of a sudden, staggered over to the man.

"I am a duck. My role is fulfilled if you kill me and serve me as food on the table," said the duck to the man the way man spoke, "but why have you imposed the sufferings upon me by throwing me in the air?"

"I thought you to be a hawk that can capture a hare," rejoined the man. "I haven't realized you are simply a duck!"

"Look at my sole. How can I catch a hare with soles like this?" laughed the duck, lifting up one of its soles to show the man.

——from *Ai Tzu's Fables*

Application

To make the best of one's power or skills, one is supposed to have a good understanding of what it is associated with, how it operates and what effect it may take. Provided you do not have so good an understanding, the power or such will not be able to bring the desired result.

猎犬毙鹰

艾子有从禽之僻，畜一猎犬，其能搏兔。艾子每出，必牵犬以自随。凡获兔，必出其心肝以与之食，莫不饫足。故凡获一兔，犬必摇尾以视艾子，自喜而待其饲也。一日出猎，偶兔少，而犬饥已甚，望草中二兔跃出，鹰翔而击之。兔狡，翻覆之际，而犬已至，乃误中其鹰，毙焉，而兔已走矣。艾子匆遽将死鹰在手，叹恨之次，犬亦如前摇尾自喜，顾艾子以待食。艾子乃顾犬而骂曰："这神狗犹自道我是哩！"

——《艾子杂说》

警言

在追求某一目标时，要保持理性，避免盲目向前。同时，也应考虑环境和条件的变化，确保在追求目标的过程中方向正确、方式合理，以取得满意的效果。

The Hunting Dog Slaying the Hawk

Ai Tzu had a hobby of hunting and kept a hunting dog or a hound, which was expert at capturing the hare. Each time Ai Tzu went hunting, he was sure to take the dog with him. As he hunted a hare, he would, with no doubt, pull out the prey's heart and livers for the dog to eat its fill. Therefore, whenever a hare was caught, the hound would gaze at its master in the belief that it would be awarded for its credit, wagging its tail and waiting to be fed the hare's heart and livers. When he went hunting one day, he chanced to come across very few hares. The dog felt starving then. All of a sudden, out of the undergrowth burst two hares, at which the hawk swooped to hit. Nonetheless, crafty were the hares, which, in struggle against the bird of prey, made the hound rush at and sink its teeth into the hawk. The bird died, and the hares darted away. Ai Tzu hurried up to the hawk, held the bird in his hands and flew into passion, when the dog, gazing upon the man, wagged its tail in the hope for his awarded share. Glaring at the dog, Ai Tzu reproached, "You stupid dog! You even think you helped!"

——from *Ai Tzu's Fables*

Application

In a bid to achieve a goal, it is vital that you stay rational instead of advancing blindly to the aim. More importantly, remind yourself of the change in conditions and the environment to make sure of the direction in which you go and the means by which you act.

囫囵吞枣

客有曰:"梨益齿而损脾,枣益脾而损齿。"

一呆弟子方思久之曰:"我食梨则嚼而不咽,不能伤我之脾;我食枣则吞而不嚼,不能伤我之齿。"

——《湛渊静语》

警言

吃有营养的食物却不细嚼细品,导致不消化、不吸收,身体没有得到裨益。在学习上如果同样食而不化,不求甚解,含糊了事,则不仅学不到知识,还浪费了时间。

Swallowing a Date Whole

"The pear is of much good to the tooth but of much harm to the spleen while the date goes the other way around," claimed someone, which happened to come to the ear of a foolish man.

Having pondered over this for a prolonged period of time, he concluded, "As I eat a pear, I will just chew it without letting it down into my stomach, in which way the pear will do no harm to my spleens. As I eat a date, I will swallow it whole without chewing it, which will bring no damage to my teeth."

——from *Miscellanea of Zhanyuan*

Application

Eating nutritious food without sufficient chewing, you are most likely to suffer from indigestion. Nourishment as you take in, you won't be brought any good by having the nutrients down into your stomach. Likewise, given that you learn knowledge but know not why or how for an improved or deepened perception of what you are fed by teachers or textbooks, you will not merely get academically well equipped but also be led to a waste of your life.

寒号鸟

五台山有鸟，名曰寒号虫。当盛暑时，文采绚烂，乃自鸣曰："凤凰不如我！"比至深冬严寒之际，毛羽脱落，索然如鷇雏，遂自鸣曰："得过且过。"

——《南村辍耕录》

警 言

目光短浅，夏不为冬谋，则冬难过。人若目光短浅，只计眼前，没有长远打算，则忧现于未来。人无远虑，必有近忧。脚踏实地地劳作，充实勤劳地度过每一个今天，才能拥有安逸无忧的将来。

The Cold-song Bird

In Mount Wutai lives a bird, called the cold-song bird, who has four feet and thick-fleshed wings and can't fly. "The phoenix is not so good as me," he says in the height of summer when his feathers take on a blaze of colour. Upon the arrival of the savage cold of late winter, he sheds his feathers, looking like a new-born chick, bald and crumpled. Now he says, let me muddle along.

——from *Miscellanea by Tao Zongyi*

Application

Eyes laid on the present season of summer but not beyond to winter, the bird has a hard winter to get through. If a man is short of sight, calculating merely what's at hand, he is sure to meet with adversity latent in the future. He who has no plan for the future must find trouble on its way to him presently. Therefore, work in a down-to-earth manner with diligence to have today full and worthy, and you will own an easy and anxiety-free future.

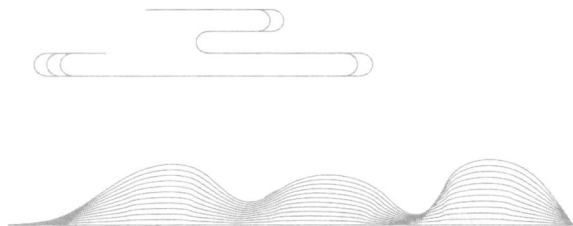

东郭先生和狼

　　赵简子大猎于中山，有狼当道，驱车逐之。时东郭先生，将北适中山以干仕，策蹇驴，囊图书，夙行失道。狼奄至，引首顾曰："先生岂有志于济物哉？何不使我早处囊中，以苟延残喘乎？异时倘得脱颖而出，先生之恩，生死而肉骨也。"先生乃出图书，空囊橐，徐徐焉实狼其中。已而简子至，求狼弗得，回车就道。狼度简子之去远，而作声囊中曰："先生可留意矣，出我囊。"先生举手出狼，狼咆哮谓先生曰："适为虞人逐，其来甚速，幸先生生我。我饿甚，馁不得食，亦终必亡而已，又何吝一躯啖我，而全微命乎！"遂鼓吻奋爪以向先生。先生仓卒以手搏之。还望老子杖藜而来，先生且喜且愕，舍狼而前，拜跪啼泣，致辞曰："乞丈人一言而生。"丈人问故。先生曰："是狼为虞人所窘，求救于我，我实生之，今反欲噬我，敢乞一言而生。"狼曰："初先生救我时，束缚我足，闭我囊中，压以诗书，我鞠躬不敢息，又蔓词以说简子，其意盖将死我于囊，而独窃其利也，吾安可不噬？"丈人曰："是皆不足以执信也！试再囊之，吾观其状，果困苦否。"狼欣然从之。丈人附耳谓先生曰："有匕首否？"先生曰："有。"于是出匕，丈人目先生使引匕刺狼。先生曰："不害狼乎！"丈人笑曰："禽兽负恩为是，而犹不忍杀，子固仁者，然愚亦甚矣！"遂举手助先生操刀，共殪狼，弃道上而去。

　　　　　　　　　　　　　　　　　　——《中山狼传》

　　施爱于善，得善；施爱于恶，恶报。"兼爱非攻"本是一种非常积极普爱的思想和行为，然而在现实世界中，若不能辨别善恶而兼爱非攻，则是盲目愚蠢的助恶行为，继而导致恶果。

The Scholar Dongguo and the Wolf

Zhao Jian Tzu, a senior official of Jin, went on hunting to the Zhongshan Mountain, where he found a wolf in the middle of the road, after which Jian Tzu chased. In the meanwhile, a scholar by the name of Dongguo was riding his lame donkey, which was loaded with a sack filled with books, on his way northward in an attempt to seek an official position. As he was hurrying off on his journey, he lost his way, hesitating in which direction to head. At this very moment, a wolf came up in fright, craned his neck and spoke to Dongguo.

"Does Your Kindness have a heart of charity?" said the wolf to Dongguo. "Why don't you let me into your sack, giving me a chance to survive? If you get me out of danger, I will for ever bear in mind your mercy on me, which brings one back to life and makes white bones regain flesh."

With these words to his ear, the scholar of compassion emptied his big bag of books, edging the wolf inside. Presently, Jian Tzu together with other hunters came over, found not the wolf and made away toward a road.

"Hello, mister. Let me out of the sack, please," demanded the wolf, who was assured of the hunters having gone far.

No sooner had Dongguo, as the wolf asked, released the beast from the sack than the latter could not wait to expose his villainy to the honest scholar.

"I was running for my life from the hunters who came to me so soon. I was lucky that Your Kindness saved my life," roared the wolf. "And now I am starving to death, having no food to eat, only to die a hungry death. Then spare not your life to save mine!"

With these words, the wolf, baring his fangs, launched himself at the kind-hearted man, who then promptly engaged in a fight against the villainous beast with might and main, bare-handed. He chanced to turn around and much to his relief, an old man eased toward him with a walking stick. Agreeably surprised, he broke away from the animal, got down on his knees and cried.

"Please save me," said the kind scholar to the old man, beggingly, who enquired what was going on between the scholar and the wolf.

"This wolf, who was stalked by hunters and got in a desperate plight, came to me for help," explained the scholar entreatingly. "But after I saved his life, he was desirous of devouring me. Please put in some words for me."

"When His Kindness tried to save me, he bound my feet, tucked me in the bag, and laid his books upon me," complained the wolf to the old man. "Curling up, I didn't dare take a breath before he ended his lengthy conversation with Jian Tzu. I bet he had the intent to smother me in the bag. In this case, why should I not devour him?"

"Your words do not suffice to illustrate your point," said the old man to both the wolf and the scholar.

"Show me how you managed to let him in such a bag," suggested the old man, "and I will know what really happened and see if it brought along suffering."

The wolf would fain do as he was asked. The old man put his mouth to the scholar's ear, and whispered a question, "Do you have a dagger?"

"Yes," replied Dongguo.

The scholar produced a dagger thereupon. The old man then winked at him, signalling to him to stab at the ignominious brute.

"Isn't this to hurt the wolf?" demurred the kind man.

"As you can't bear to kill so ungrateful a beast, you are indeed a beneficent man," laughed the old man. "However, it's foolish of you."

Thereby the old man put the dagger to the joint hold of Dongguo and himself. The two men pushed the dagger into the wolf together, deserted the animal where he was and made their way on.

——from *Story of the Wolf of the Zhongshan Mountain*

Application

Bestow love upon those who are kind, and you will be well returned; bestow love upon those who are wicked, and you will be badly returned. Philanthropy with non-aggression, as a matter of fact, is a positive thought and conduct. Nonetheless, in the real world, kindness and viciousness not discerned, blind bestowal of love, which may lead to villainy, is likely to put kind-heartedness to an unagreeable end.

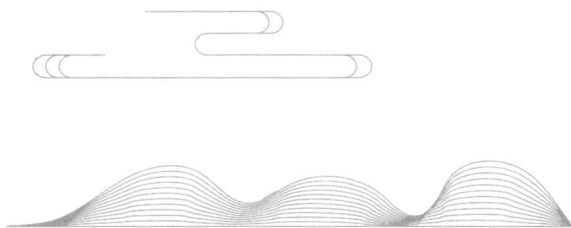

铁杵磨成针

李白少读书，未成，弃去。道逢老妪磨杵，白问其故。曰："欲作针。"白笑其拙，老妇曰："功到自然成耳。"白感其言，遂卒业。

——《潜确类书》

警言

无论是在学习上还是在事业二，不论是否具有天赋才华，下苦功夫、坚持不懈都是通往成功的必经之路。

Grinding an Iron Pestle into a Needle

As a boy, Li Bai quitted school in the middle of his studies. Once in the street he came across an elderly woman, who was rubbing an iron pestle on a stone. Seeing this, Bai stepped over and enquired what she was doing with the pestle being ground against the stone.

"To transform it into a needle with which to sew," replied the aged one.

"It's stupid of you to attempt to grind a pestle like this down to a tiny needle," laughed the child.

"My enduring work of rubbing will bring a big pestle to its transformation into a sewing needle," protested the old woman.

Stirred by her inspiring utterance, Li Bai went on with his schooling and completed his studies.

——from *Miscellanea Collected by Chen Renxi*

Application

In terms of studies or career building, no matter whether you have a gift for what you aspire to, constant effort or persistence is the only access to your desired achievement.

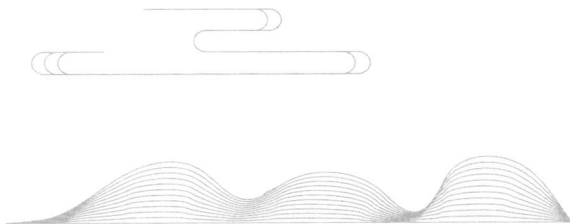

翠鸟移巢

翠鸟先高作巢以避患。及生子,爱之,恐坠,稍下作巢。子长羽毛,复益爱之,又更下巢,而人遂得而取之矣。

——《古今谭概》

警 言

这则寓言告诉我们,对孩子过分的溺爱和保护会使他们在面对危机时不知所措,不知道该如何去独立面对生活的挑战。

The Kingfisher Moving Down Nest

The kingfisher, timid and cautious, builds her nest high up in the tree against any possible danger or threat. As her chicks hatch, the kingfisher, who loves her babies, moves the nest a bit lower in the tree for fear that they might slip down to the ground, hurt. When they fledge, the bird, who is in more love with her progeny, brings the nest down even lower in the tree for the same concern she has over her offspring. And this has made the nest accessible to any human being who attempts bird capture.

——from *Miscellaneous Analects*

Application

This fable warns us not to allow our children too much care, protection or attention, which may deprive them of the access to basic survival skills to dispose of the likely crises or meet challenges in life.

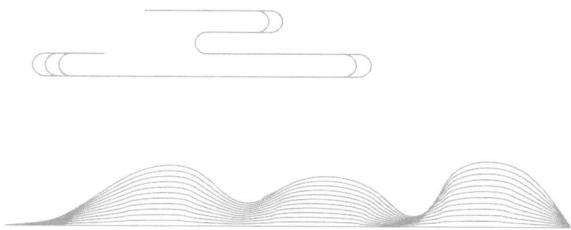

猩猩醉酒

山谷间，常数十为群。里人以酒并糟设于路侧，织草为屦，更相连结。猩猩见酒及屦，知里人设张，则知张者祖先姓字，乃呼名云："奴欲张我！"舍而去。后自再三，相谓曰："试共尝酒。"及饮其味，逮乎醉。因取屦着之而踬。乃为人擒，无遗者。

——《古今谭概》

警言

贪则智昏，不计后果；贪则胆大，胆大则妄为。贪之际，则祸福无分。

The Drunken Baboons

In a valley live baboons that come and go in groups of scores. The local people, in the knowledge of the primates' habits and characteristics, lay wine dregs and straw sandals stringed on a line by the roadside. At the sight of the wine and sandals, the clever animals are aware that it is a trap that the locals set and even know their ancestors' names. The baboons thereby cry out their names and "You want to trap me!" clamour they. With these words, they resist the temptation and turn tail. The same trap is set like that many a time until they make an attempt to persuade each other, "Let's try a mouthful." As they have savoured the wine, they can't help drinking without stop until they get dead drunk. At this point, they put on the sandals, trip and fall. Thereupon the people approach and capture them.

——from *Miscellaneous Analects*

Application

Voracity leads to muddleheadedness, followed by recklessness; voracity leads to audacity, after which wild acts ensue. Overwhelmed by this inner desire, one will be unable to distinguish weal from woe.

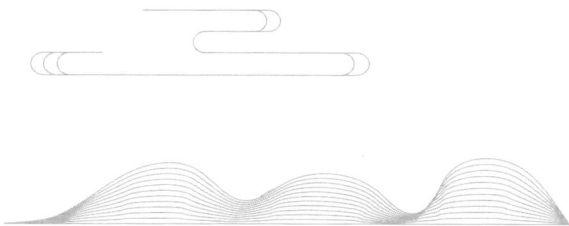

姜结于树

楚人有生而不识姜者，曰："此从树上结成。"

或曰："从土里生成。"

其人固执己见，曰："请与子以十人为质，以所乘驴为赌。"

已而遍问十人，皆曰："土里生也。"

其人哑然失色，曰："驴则付汝，姜还树生。"

——《雪涛小说》

警言

应尊重客观事实，谦虚谨慎，善于倾听建议，明辨真伪，勇于承认自己的错误，不应固执己见。固执己见，可能导致失败和挫折。

The Ginger Grows on the Tree

In the state of Chu lived a man, who did not have an iota of knowledge of the ginger, let alone where it grew.

"The ginger grows on the tree," he claimed.

"Nope. It grows in the soil," protested someone else.

Adhering much to his own opinion, the man argued, "Let's enquire ten people about where the ginger grows. I will bet my donkey on this with you."

A short while later, the two men who lay the bet enquired ten men, who unanimously replied that the ginger was from the ground.

The one who knew not the ginger turned cross. "Just take the donkey," mumbled the man, protestingly. "All the same, the ginger is nothing but grows on the tree."

——from *Stories by Xue Tao*

Application

As is considered important, we should show respect for what the fact is like, be modest about what we have little knowledge of, keep ears open to those who know better or who are wiser, discern right from wrong, and more importantly, admit the mistakes we have made without stubbornly sticking to our own opinion. If we fail to do that, we may subside to failure or setbacks.

蚕与蛛

　　蛛语蚕曰:"尔饱食终日以至于老,口吐经纬,黄口灿然,固之自裹。蚕妇操汝入于沸汤,抽为长丝乃丧厥躯。然则其巧也,适以自杀,不亦愚乎!"

　　蚕答蛛曰:"我固自杀。我所吐者,遂为文竟,天子衮口龙,百官绂绣,孰非我为? 汝乃枵腹而营口吐经纬,织成网罗,坐伺其间,蚊虻蜂蝶之见过者无不杀之,而以自饱。巧则巧矣何其忍也!"蛛曰:"为人谋则为汝自谋,宁为我!"噫,世之为蚕不为蛛者寡矣夫!

——《雪涛小说》

警 言

　　蚕和蜘蛛带来了两种不同的人生观:为人或为己。蚕的自我牺牲精神,为人们所称颂,而蛛则自私自利。蚕的自我牺牲精神,值得人去学习。

The Silkworm and the Spider

"You stuff yourself daily with mulberry leaves until you come to the end of your life, producing weaving thread of shining gold, with which you spin a cocoon to trap in yourself," the Spider said to the Silkworm. "Silkworm-raising women steep you in boiling water, and draw the long silk out of your cocoon, ruining your home and body. It is just the stunt of yours to produce thread that makes the means of slaying yourself. Isn't it stupid?"

"It is true that the way I live is the way to death. However, the silk I produce can be woven into silk cloth. From the emperor's dress with the patterns of the dragon to the officials' court dress, which is NOT made of the silk I produced?" replied the Silkworm. "You have the knack of spinning silk, on which you wait for prey. Whatever comes in your sight, mosquitoes, small insects, bees and butterflies, you will spare none of their lives for your meal. Well-designed as your web is, what cruelty it has brought about!"

"One would choose to be you if he thinks more of others while he would choose to be me if he has more considerations of himself," concluded the Spider.

Alas, those who are desirous of being the Silkworm are fewer than those who aspire to be the Spider!

———from *Stories by Xue Tao*

Application

The Silkworm and the Spider have stated two distinct views of life: self-sacrifice or sacrifice of others. The self-sacrifice of the Silkworm has been in the eulogy of man, with the selfishness of the Spider spared as a subject of conversation.

医驼背

昔有医人,自媒能治背驼,曰:"如弓者、如虾者、如曲环者,延吾治,可朝治而夕如矢。"一人信焉,而使治驼。乃索板二片,以一置地下,卧驼者其上,又以一压焉,而即屣焉,驼者随直,亦复随死。

其子欲鸣诸官,医人曰:"我业治驼,但管人直,那管人死!"

——《雪涛小说》

警 言

主观意愿未必通往期待的结果。处理问题时,若未能结合实际情况并采取科学的方法,则会导致严重的后果。

Treating Deformities of the Back

There was once a charlatan who claimed he could cure deformed backs by chiropractic treatment.

"Bent like a bow, a shrimp, or a ring, your back will be as straight as the arrow on the very night if you come to me in the morning," clamoured the fake doctor.

A hunchback believed the words, letting the doctor exert the treatment on the physical deformity of his back. The charlatan sought two planks, put one on the ground and made the hunchback prostrate on it before he pressed the other over the hump. After all done, the doctor trod up and down on the upper plank until the hump went straight. However, the man who sought chiropractic treatment was trampled to death.

To his utmost fury, the man's son desired to charge him with the fraud. "My job is to treat deformities of the back, and so I did. To complete my job, whether or not the man dies is not to my care!" the charlatan demurred.

——from *Stories by Xue Tao*

Application

Expectations may not lead to the expected consequence, which deviates oftentimes from man's will. When an issue is attended to, measures or methods that are divorced from realities may bring the issue to a severe result.

神像和好人

　　乡村路口,有一神庙,乃是木雕之像。一人行路,因遇水沟,就将此神放倒,踏着过水。后有一人看见,心内不忍,将神扶在座上。

　　此神说他不供香火,登时就降他头痛之灾。

　　判官小鬼都禀道:"踏着大王过水的倒没事,扶起来的倒降灾,何也?"

　　这神说:"你不知道,只是善人好欺负。"

——《笑赞》

警 言

　　人之恶之一,便是欺善。世间事,道不清,本应以善应善,却总是会以恶应善。这则寓言警示我们,此种以恶报善实属不该,以善应善才是为人正道。

An Idol and a Good Man

A man went past a wooden idol that sat on the village altar set by the roadside. Trying to get over a puddle along the path, the man took the idol off the shrine and laid it over the puddle on which he stepped. Another passer-by, found the figure on the ground, couldn't bear to see it subjected to trampling on the ground and then restored it to its seat.

The idol took umbrage, claimed that the man offered no sacrifice to it and cast a spell of headache on him then and there.

"You let go of the one who trod on you, but put a curse on the one who helped you back to the shrine. Why is that?" stated the judge and other spirits of the netherworld, confounded.

"As you don't know," explained the idol, "it is a pushover to bully a nice man."

——from *A Collection of Satirical Jokes*

Application

As one can hardly imagine, one of man's evil qualities is to bully the good man. Of great complexity is the way to act in the mortal world, where virtue that should be returned with good deeds oftentimes comes across a bad return. This fable warns us to take the right way of righting the wrong in a bid to spread virtue and not to let down those who exert beneficence.

· 参考文献 ·

[1] 白珽. 湛渊静语[M]. 北京：中华书局，1985.

[2] 班固. 汉书[M]. 颜师古，注. 北京：中华书局，2012.

[3] 陈蒲清. 序[M]//杨宪益，戴乃迭，英译. 中国古代寓言选. 北京：外文出版社，2008：1-3.

[4] 陈仁锡. 潜确类书（本衙藏版）[M]. 陈明卿太史纂辑. 明代.

[5] 冯梦龙. 古今谭概[M]. 栾保群，点校. 北京：中华书局，2007.

[6] 韩非. 韩非子[M]. 高华平，王齐洲，张三夕，译注. 北京：中华书局，2010.

[7] 江盈科. 雪涛小说[M]. 黄仁生，校注. 上海：上海古籍出版社，2000.

[8] 列御寇. 列子[M]. 叶蓓卿，译注. 北京：中华书局，2011.

[9] 刘安. 淮南子[M]. 陈广忠，译注. 北京：中华书局，2012.

[10] 刘向. 新序[M]. 马世年，译注. 北京：中华书局，2014.

[11] 刘向. 战国策[M]. 缪文远，缪伟，罗永莲，译注. 北京：中华书局，2012.

[12] 刘向. 说苑[M]. 王天海，杨秀岚，译注. 北京：中华书局，2019.

[13] 柳宗元. 柳河东集[M]. 上海：上海人民出版社，1974.

[14] 吕不韦. 吕氏春秋[M]. 张双隶，张万彬，殷国光，陈涛，译注. 北京：中华书局，2011.

[15] 孟轲. 孟子[M]. 方勇，译注. 北京：中华书局，2010.

[16] 商鞅. 商君书[M]. 石磊，译注. 北京：中华书局，2011.

[17] 苏轼. 艾子杂说[M]. 北京：中华书局，1985.

[18] 陶宗仪. 南村辍耕录[M]. 上海：上海古籍出版社，2012.

[19] 王安石. 临川先生文集[M]. 北京:国家图书出版社,2018.

[20] 荀况. 荀子[M]. 方勇,李波,译注. 北京:中华书局,2011.

[21] 晏婴. 晏子春秋[M]. 汤化,译注. 北京:中华书局,2011.

[22] 应劭. 风俗通义[M]. 孙雪霞,陈桐生,译注. 北京:中华书局,
2021.

[23] 杨宪益,戴乃迭 英译. 中国古代寓言选[M]. 滕一岚,今译.
北京:外文出版社,2008.

[24] 杨雄. 法言[M]. 韩敬,译注. 北京:中华书局,

[25] 庄周. 庄子[M]. 方勇,译注. 北京:中华书局,2010.